THE FEINT

There was only the one shot. Yet Raider heard no slug sizzle past his ear, heard no whining, quavering song of ricochet...

He looked toward his horse.

Oh, shit, Raider thought.

For the first time he felt a clenching of fear deep in his gut.

The horse was not peering out toward some gunman. It stood head down and spraddle-legged, fighting a losing battle to maintain its balance. Strings of pale snot hung down from its nostrils. And—nearly black in the dim light—blood.

All caution abandoned, Raider lurched to his feet, his heart pounding furiously.

Because there was only one reason for anyone to pull him away and then shoot his horse.

And that reason was Lucinda McCollum.

Raider ran through the night. He ran with a cold, hopeless fury lying icy and knotted in his gut...

Other books by
J.D. HARDIN

- BLOOD, SWEAT AND GOLD
- THE GOOD, THE BAD, AND THE DEADLY
- THE SLICK AND THE DEAD
- BULLETS, BUZZARDS, BOXES OF PINE
- FACE DOWN IN A COFFIN
- THE MAN WHO BIT SNAKES
- THE SPIRIT AND THE FLESH
- BLOODY SANDS
- RAIDER'S HELL
- RAIDER'S REVENGE
- HARD CHAINS, SOFT WOMEN
- RAIDER'S GOLD
- SILVER TOMBSTONES
- DEATH LODE
- COLDHEARTED LADY
- GUNFIRE AT SPANISH ROCK
- SONS AND SINNERS
- DEATH FLOTILLA
- SNAKE RIVER RESCUE
- THE LONE STAR MASSACRE
- BOBBIES, BAUBLES AND BLOOD
- BIBLES, BULLETS AND BRIDES
- HELLFIRE HIDEAWAY
- APACHE GOLD
- SASKATCHEWAN RISING
- HANGMAN'S NOOSE
- BLOODY TIME IN BLACKTOWER
- THE MAN WITH NO FACE
- THE FIREBRANDS
- DOWNRIVER TO HELL
- BOUNTY HUNTER
- QUEENS OVER DEUCES
- CARNIVAL OF DEATH
- SATAN'S BARGAIN
- THE WYOMING SPECIAL
- LEAD-LINED COFFINS
- SAN JUAN SHOOT-OUT
- THE PECOS DOLLARS
- VENGEANCE VALLEY
- OUTLAW TRAIL
- HOMESTEADER'S REVENGE
- TOMBSTONE IN DEADWOOD
- THE OZARK OUTLAWS
- COLORADO SILVER QUEEN
- THE BUFFALO SOLDIER
- THE GREAT JEWEL ROBBERY
- THE COCHISE COUNTY WAR
- APACHE TRAIL
- IN THE HEART OF TEXAS
- THE COLORADO STING
- HELL'S BELLE
- CATTLETOWN WAR
- THE GHOST MINE
- MAXIMILIAN'S GOLD
- THE TINCUP RAILROAD WAR
- CARSON CITY COLT
- GUNS AT BUZZARD BEND
- THE RUNAWAY RANCHER
- THE LONGEST MANHUNT
- THE NORTHLAND MARAUDERS
- BLOOD IN THE BIG HATCHETS
- THE GENTLEMAN BRAWLER
- MURDER ON THE RAILS
- IRON TRAIL TO DEATH
- THE FORT WORTH CATTLE MYSTERY
- THE ALAMO TREASURE
- BREWER'S WAR
- THE SWINDLER'S TRAIL
- THE BLACK HILLS SHOWDOWN

J.D. HARDIN
SAVAGE REVENGE

BERKLEY BOOKS, NEW YORK

SAVAGE REVENGE

A Berkley Book/published by arrangement with
the author

PRINTING HISTORY
Berkley edition/March 1987

All rights reserved.
Copyright © 1987 by J. D. Hardin.
This book may not be reproduced in whole or in part,
by mimeograph or any other means, without permission.
For information address: The Berkley Publishing Group,
200 Madison Avenue, New York, N.Y. 10016.

ISBN: 0-425-09648-3

A BERKLEY BOOK ® TM 757,375
Berkley Books are published by The Berkley Publishing Group,
200 Madison Avenue, New York, N.Y. 10016.
The name "BERKLEY" and the stylized "B" with design are
trademarks belonging to Berkley Publishing Corporation.

PRINTED IN THE UNITED STATES OF AMERICA

CHAPTER ONE

Raider stretched, his eyes still closed, enjoying immensely the weight of the warm blanket that was pulled over him chin high. And the warmth of the woman who lay at his side.

As little as his waking movement had been, it was enough to bring her out of her night's sleep too. She rolled dreamily onto her side and burrowed backward against him, cupping the round swell of her buttocks against his groin. His arm slipped over her, and he found the soft mound of her breast, lightly stroking and squeezing it.

His erection was hard and insistent against her backside, and after a moment he fumbled for the hem of her sleeping gown, raising it to her waist so there was no barrier between them.

"Wait," she whispered. He could feel her raise her head. He didn't have to see her to know what she was doing. She was checking to make sure that the boy was still asleep in his bunk on the far side of the room.

After a moment she laid her head back onto the pillow and wordlessly reached down between her thighs to find and to guide him.

Almost without either of them having to change position, he slid inside her and they lay there joined, back to belly, buttocks to groin, as Raider enjoyed the warm, moist depths of her body.

They lay like that for a minute or more, unmoving, accepting the quiet pleasures of the moment. Then Raider let his hand roam under her gown to find and fondle her left nipple while very slowly and cautiously he began to stroke in and out of her. Lucinda uttered a very faint murmur of pleasure and pressed herself closer against him.

Raider kissed the back of her neck and squeezed her breast tighter, but his movements continued to be very slow and gentle. They had to be quiet and careful because the ropes that suspended the grass-filled ticking mattress in the homemade bed tended to creak, and he didn't want to wake the boy. It was enough that the kid was asked to accept the fact that Raider had moved in with them. It would have been embarrassing to know that the youngster was listening to the pleasures Raider took with his mother.

Oddly, the enforced stealth of those morning pleasures seemed to heighten the feeling of it. Instead of being restrictive, the need for silence lent spice to the couplings. Raider didn't fully understand that, but he was more than willing to accept it.

Already he could feel a growing rush of sensation deep in his balls. He slowed his quiet stroking even more, not wanting it to end yet.

Lucinda wriggled against him in silent protest. Smiling, Raider trailed his fingertips down across the slight bulge of her belly, into the tangle of dark hair, until he found the wet, lightly pulsing upper end of her opening. He began to stroke her button of joy with a finger while he continued to move in and out of her.

He could feel the quickening of her breath as she responded to his touch. Her head drew back, the tendons in her slender neck as tight as a strung bow, and her lips were pulled away from her teeth in a grimace that could have been mistaken for pain but was not.

He felt her stiffen and shudder, pressing herself back against him wantonly.

He knew she wanted to cry out. When they were alone, when they didn't have to worry about the boy hearing, she was prone to loud squeals and cries at this moment.

He could feel the walls of her sex contract, tightening like clamps around the base of his cock as she struggled to contain the moans that welled up inside her throat.

That last bit of sensation was more than he could overcome. He lost his battle to hold back—not that he was fighting it all that much now—and muffled his ecstatic grunt of satisfaction against Lucinda's warm flesh.

He pressed forward, deep inside her, so that the sensitive base of his cock was pushed hard against her pelvic bone. The effect was to limit the flow of his seed, slowing it and prolonging the already exquisite sensation, bringing his sense of pleasure to an almost unbearable level from the long, slow climax.

Lucinda sighed and went limp against him, her satisfaction fully as complete as his had been.

She turned her head to kiss him, and Raider held her close. He felt an unfamiliar tightness in his throat and a welling up of feeling for this woman that had nothing to do with the enjoyment he found in her body.

The feeling, whatever it might be called, went far beyond that.

It was something that was new to him. He was not entirely sure that he liked it.

In a way it was frightening—beyond his control and even uncomfortable.

But he could not deny it. He was not sure that he wanted to.

"G'morning." It was the boy. He sat up, his blankets falling away from his skinny torso, and began to rub at his eyes. But already, not even fully awake yet, he was grinning and happy with the new day that was starting.

"Good morning, honey." Deftly Lucinda disengaged herself from Raider's flaccid cock and pushed her gown down to cover herself before she slipped out from under the covers and went to start the fire and begin cooking their breakfast.

Raider winked at the kid and smiled. The day was begun, and he was looking forward to it every bit as much as the boy was, by damn. He waited until the kid had stepped into his overalls and made his early morning dash for the backhouse before Raider reached for his drawers and climbed out of the bed. By then Lucinda had water on the stove to heat for coffee and was already mixing batter for the corncake that would be the morning meal.

This was good, Raider silently acknowledged. This was a glimpse of a life he had never really known before, and he liked it.

CHAPTER TWO

Weatherbee touched the starched white linen napkin to his lips, patting delicately. He hesitated for a moment, then succumbed to the temptation of the plate of hors d'oeuvres being passed by a red-jacketed waiter. A few more would do no harm.

He munched with pleasure on the crustless finger sandwiches, one a combination of olives with soft cheese, the other watercress with a delightfully tangy mayonnaise. The chef who had concocted such a mayonnaise was to be complimented. Doc had rarely tasted better.

Another waiter moved fluidly past, and Doc helped himself to a long-stemmed glass of champagne.

He leaned against a pillar along the south end of the ballroom and sipped at his glass, quite thoroughly content with the evening, the guests, indeed with the whole of this vacation.

The ballroom of the Antlers was every bit as grand as anything Weatherbee might have expected to find back in his native Boston, from the parquet floor to the ornately gilded ceiling.

And the guests this evening were as gay and sparkling as were the crystal chandeliers overhead—chandeliers that were, in fact, electrified. Gas lamps contributed a soft, warm glow of yellow-white from the wall fixtures, but the chandeliers were entirely electric. The only candles in evidence throughout the whole huge room were those that danced and fluttered in the table centerpieces, each arrangement made with sprays of brightly golden aspen leaves. The foliage had to have been gathered from some high, if not necessarily distant, elevation, perhaps from the flanks of Pikes Peak, which looked down with benign dignity on the Antlers Hotel and General Palmer's elegant community.

The general's foresight and industry—and wealth—had created here a community that was as gracious as any one could hope for. It was indeed the Paris of the West.

Weatherbee finished his champagne and set the empty glass onto a tray offered by an observant waiter, then declined another glass.

His attention was not on food and drink at the moment but on a particular lady across the great room.

Emilie von Hausen was likely ten years or more past her own coming out, yet she was surrounded by an admiring bevy of the current season's debutantes, each of whom would have been well served if they could learn to ape her style and grace. And surrounded as well, if from a slightly greater distance, by a group of overeager young swains in evening clothes and with silly grins plastered on their faces.

Doc's lips tightened briefly, the only outward sign of the amusement he felt at this moment. There likely was not a one among those youthful male admirers who would not willingly pledge himself Emilie's eternal slave in exchange for a touch of the lady's lips. Even for her merest smile.

Ah, how little they knew, Doc thought. How very much they had yet to learn. There was no power on earth that could force him to travel that long and painful route of learning a second time. He had had to endure it once; that had been more than enough for any one lifetime.

Nor were the young the only ones to live in delusion. A gentleman with muttonchop whiskers, a huge belly, and suspiciously dark hair stopped in front of the group, bent low over Emilie's gloved hand, and spoke. Her response was smiles and laughter and a few softly spoken words. Doc did not have to hear what she was saying to guess the content. The gentleman, who was said to control half the timber and three-quarters of the shipping on the northwestern coast, bowed a second time. And then beat a *very* hasty retreat to the far side of the ballroom floor.

This time Doc's smile was open, if brief.

He could hear the faint shuffle and clatter as musicians filed back into the room after their intermission. The dancing would start again soon, and Doc looked about for a suitable partner, someone not too young and not too pretty. A partner safe and uncomplicated and about whom no whispers would attach.

Perfect. Lady Jane Hawes was unattended. Lady Jane was horse-faced and fortyish, to all appearances more interested in the horses she resembled than in male companionship. Which Doc could understand, having made the acquaintance of Lord Hawes, who was this evening indisposed by the gout. Doc turned toward her but was interrupted by a touch on his elbow.

"Weatherbee, old fellow. Been lookin' for you everywhere."

"Yes, Donald?" Weatherbee recognized the chap. Donald Lampkin was from Cambridge—Massachusetts, not England—and spoke with an affected British accent. Lampkin had been two terms behind Doc at Harvard, where they had been passingly acquainted if not exactly friends.

Nowadays Lampkin had something to do with his father's brokerage house. Just what it was he did with the firm was unclear. Except, of course, for drawing a salary.

"We've a smashing group assembling to picnic tomorrow, Weatherbee. Carriages to the Garden of the Gods. Caterer to meet us there. All o' that. Thought you might want to join us."

It sounded pleasant enough until Lampkin winked and added, "The ladies will be, um, not entirely of the best sort, if you get my meaning, Weatherbee." Lampkin winked again and nudged Doc in the side with an elbow.

Which meant that Lampkin, whose wife was somewhere off touring the Continent this year, was gathering up a bunch of hale fellows to go whoring with him. Weatherbee resented the implication but did not let that show. Instead he grimaced with apparent regret and explained, "I wish you had caught me half an hour earlier, Donald. I'm afraid I have an engagement already."

"Pity, eh, Weatherbee? Next time, what?"

"Uh, next time. Of course."

Lampkin excused himself and hurried on toward a group of gentlemen who were unaccompanied by ladies. Doc shook his head slightly. He never could understand the compulsion of some men to publicly proclaim revels that they quite possibly could not accomplish in private. Or perhaps that itself was reason enough for the activity.

He drifted along the wall until he reached Lady Jane, who was in conversation with an elderly and quite elegantly dressed woman.

"My dear man, I should be delighted," Lady Jane squealed when Doc extended an invitation for the dance. The orchestra had finished tuning their strings now and were preparing for the opening waltz of the set. Lady Jane took Doc's arm and accompanied him onto the quickly filling floor.

"So kind of you to ask me, dear boy," she said as she moved *much* closer to him than custom warranted. The dance began, and Doc could repeatedly feel the brush of her breasts against his lapels. The slight contact was doing nothing for him, but unless he was terribly mistaken there was now an elongation of Lady Jane's nipples behind the bodice of her gown.

And she had the most curious expression on her long, homely face.

Doc glanced briefly across the crowded floor, toward where Emilie was dancing now with one of the grinning, nameless youngsters who politely clamored for her attentions. He looked back toward Lady Jane Hawes, whose cheeks were quite suddenly flushed with emotion.

And wondered if he had inadvertently bitten off more here than he wanted to chew.

CHAPTER THREE

"Hold him now, hold him. That's right. You're doing just fine. Keep him still." Raider accepted the hot iron Lucinda brought from the fire and bent over the bull calf. The calf kicked and bellowed as the gray-white tip of the iron burned through the layer of hair to sear onto its flesh the Rafter L brand that Raider slowly drew.

"Perfect, Kenny. You're doing just right. Keep him there just another minute." Raider handed the branding iron back to Lucinda—it was her job to tend the fire and the running irons that were jammed deep into the coals—and picked up the paring knife he had borrowed from Lucinda's kitchen. "Just another little bit now, Kenny."

The boy was having difficulty holding the calf. The bull, after all, probably outweighted him by a good twenty pounds. Still, the frail eleven-year-old was no shirker. And he seemed to be proud of the job Raider had given him.

Kenny had a death grip on the bull calf's tail, holding it between the struggling animal's back legs and applying his whole weight, little though that was, to the calf's hocks. As long as the calf could not control its hind legs it could not rise, no matter how much thrashing and effort it made with its head and forelegs. It had taken Kenny a few kicks to the head to realize the truth of what Raider had told him. Now he knew enough to brace his chest against the calf's back hocks, too close to the front quarters for those frantic kicks to reach him.

"That's it, kid." Raider grinned encouragement at him.

"You're gonna be a helluva mugger once you get some more beef on you."

The boy grinned back at him. A scrape beside his left ear looked painful. It was almost as bright red as the carroty color of his unruly hair. But it had not been enough to make him cry or make him quit. He took the lump and learned from it.

Raider knelt in the manure-stained dirt behind the calf. He took the little bull by the scrotum. Two quick slices with the knife blade, a squeeze and a final cut to separate the cords, and the bull had become a steer. Raider palmed the pale, shiny testes, and Kenny let the bawling calf up, jumping quickly aside as the thoroughly frightened calf let out a final kick of protest and ran for the safety of its mother's side.

"Am I gettin' it?" Kenny asked.

Raider nodded solemnly. "Just right that time. I couldn't have done it better myself."

The boy beamed his pleasure at the compliment and brushed the dirt from his hands—although really it was his trousers that needed the cleaning. The calves tended to squirt streams of runny shit when they were branded, and before this day was done both Kenny and Raider would be wearing britches that would be hard-crusted with dried manure.

Lucinda held out a tin pail that once had held lard, and Raider dropped the pair of elongated testes in with the others they had already collected. Sliced, lightly floured, and fried, they would make a fitting reward at suppertime for a long and difficult day of work.

"Ready for another one?" Raider asked.

"You bet." Kenny hesitated for only a moment. "But make it a heifer this time, will ya?"

Raider laughed. The kid was no dummy. It was easier to handle the heifers. They only had to be held down long enough for the brand to be applied. He didn't miss either that the boy was calling the young females heifers now. When they started this morning the youngster had still been referring to them as "girl cows." One correction and he was calling them heifers. Kenny was all right.

Raider ruffled the boy's hair, then turned to the saddled horse that was patiently waiting on a ground rein nearby.

With only the three of them to do the branding, and Raider the only grown man in the crew, it was Raider's job to rope the calves out of the pen and bring them to where Kenny could throw—and hadn't it been a kick watching the boy learn to do *that*—and hold them while Raider dismounted and took care of the branding and any necessary castration.

Still, they were learning how to work together and get it done. Working together right damned well, Raider thought.

In fact, he was willing to say that the three of them made a pretty damn good team.

And it wasn't as if Lucinda had so many cows that the three of them couldn't handle the branding. That day would come in time, of course, as the newly founded ranch prospered and grew, but that time was years away still.

He stepped onto the horse and gave Lucinda a wink, as much promise as approval, while he shook out his rope and prepared his loop for a throw.

She opened the gate of the pen Raider had built earlier in the week, and Raider rode into the small herd, his lean body swaying with the horse's motion while the two of them picked out the next calf that would be dragged to the branding fire.

CHAPTER FOUR

Weatherbee splashed some sweet-scented Pinaud Clubman into his palm, hesitated, then added some more. He rubbed his hands together briefly, then wiped the scent over his freshly shaven cheeks, on his chest and—judiciously—inside his upper thighs. There was no telling where the rest of the evening might lead, and he was taking no chances.

Despite the late hour, he felt fresh and vigorous. It had been past ten before he slipped away from the soiree downstairs, but now, after a bath and a quick shave, he felt rested and ready to go again.

He paused for a moment, decided against using any more of the scent, and reached for his shirt. He was interrupted by a soft tapping at his hotel door.

"Yes?"

There was no immediate answer. He pulled the shirt on and, leaving it hanging loose and unbuttoned, crossed the room. He had no hesitation about opening the door to his caller. After all, he was on vacation here. There seemed no need for the usual cautions of his occupation. No one could know he was here. Even the Pinkerton Agency had not bothered this time to ask where he intended to spend his free time.

"Yes?" he asked again as he pulled the door open.

He blanched. Lady Jane Hawes was there. Looking quite nervous, her long, wrinkled neck twisting and turning as she tried to look in both directions down the empty hallway. "My word," Weatherbee blurted.

Lady Hawes seemed almost in a panic as she burst past him into the privacy of his room. Without taking time for conscious thought, Doc pushed the door closed behind her.

For an instant he thought something must be wrong with Lord Hawes for her to seem so harried. But surely the old gentleman cold not be in any physical difficulty from a simple touch of the gout.

Besides, Doc happened to know that the Hawes suite was two floors above Doc's relatively simple room. Any medical emergency could more easily have been handled by way of the bellcord that would have summoned instant assistance from the hotel staff.

"Lady—" He did not have time to finish the question. And as quickly he had no further questions. The purpose of Lady Jane Hawes's late-night visit became apparent when the unattractive woman threw herself against Doc's half-naked torso and pressed her mouth inexpertly against his.

He was startled. The only thing he could think of for the moment was that the poor, dreary woman had just eaten a mint, obviously to freshen her breath. He could taste it on her lumpy, probing tongue.

By then Lady Hawes's hands were busy caressing his back, sliding around to the front of his chest, clutching, demanding, and eager; finally dropping to the waistband of his trousers, where they began to fumble at the buttons of his fly.

Doc blinked and stiffened—his back, not his pecker; he certainly felt no attraction toward the woman—and tried to turn away.

Lady Hawes grasped at him and once again intruded her tongue into his mouth. When she pulled her face away from his she was actually gasping. Panting, to be more accurate about it.

Weatherbee was perplexed. At least he had had a moment to adjust his thoughts to this unexpected situation. He did not want to hurt the poor creature's feelings. But . . .

Too late. Lady Hawes moved backward, a step and then another. For a moment Doc thought it was going to be all right, that she was coming to her senses and would leave now with no more harm done than a bit of embarrassment.

Not so.

Panting still, her face flushed and neck wattles pale, she began to disrobe with frantic speed. Doc watched helplessly, distantly amazed that she could get out of so much clothing with so little time and seeming effort. Surely this could not be a practiced speed. He did not believe that for a minute.

He joined her in blushing as she displayed her body for him.

Hers was not exactly the most desirable feminine form he had lately seen.

Her figure was thick at waist and ankles, and her legs were covered with coarse, dark hair that stood out in bold contrast to the mottled, fish-belly paleness of her skin. Her thighs were muscular enough for countless hours in the saddle, but at the juncture of hip and thigh she had fatty protuberances thick enough to give her the appearance of wearing flesh-toned saddlebags. Her unsupported breasts were flabby, pendulous things that flowed down across a well-padded belly. The nipples, though, were exceptionally long. And exceptionally hard erect. Her pubic hair was dark and thick and already glistening with the moisture of anticipation.

Doc stiffened again—his shoulders, not his cock—and recognized the inevitable.

If he should reject her now, *after* having been so boldly shown the lady's all, the woman would be devastated. Literally. Rejection now would shatter every scrap of pride or self-respect the poor thing might retain after so abrupt an offering.

Doc squeezed his eyes shut for a moment. And reached out towards her.

With a gasp of excitement, Lady Jane Hawes flung herself into Weatherbee's arms with such force that she damn near knocked both of them backward onto Doc's bed.

A moment later and that would not have mattered anyway. Doc pulled her onto the down-filled mattress with him. She lay half atop him, her mouth pressed hungrily against the side of his neck and her pale, dark-veined breasts spreading like warm pap over the hard planes of his chest.

Tentatively, Doc reached down to slip a hand between her thighs. She moaned and eagerly opened herself to him.

On top of everything else, damnit, the woman smelled bad. No one seemed to have bothered to teach the lady elementary hygiene. She smelled like a dead fish.

Lady Hawes noticed nothing of Doc's discomfort, though. She had his cock wrapped in both hands and was kneading at it with sharp, quite painful grasps and pullings, an action close akin to the milking of a goat.

Doc was grateful to discover, though, that the manipulations were at least having their desired effect.

In spite of himself he was beginning to grow hard under her painful touch.

He was going to be able to perform after all.

He rolled the woman onto her back and had to hurry to keep up with her as she stuffed his erection inside the wet folds of her sex.

He was going to have to take another bath, a quick one this time, Doc was thinking as he mechanically began to pump and hump in response to the woman's urgings.

And probably use some more of the Clubman, he thought.

Lady Hawes moaned loudly into his right ear.

He wished he could see his watch, but it was lying on the bureau across the room.

She clamped those big, powerful thighs tight around him and bucked furiously in response to his entry.

Let's see, it was probably near eleven by now.

The woman's contractions rippling around the base of his cock nearly distracted him.

Emilie was expecting him by a quarter after. A few minutes delay would not hurt.

Lady Hawes cried aloud and clamped her teeth into the slab of muscle where his neck and shoulder joined.

He would have to think of some excuse to leave, of course. Or better yet to get the Hawes woman to leave his room. Concern for her reputation and her husband's well-being? That should do it, he decided.

He smiled to himself. Lady Hawes saw the expression and misinterpreted it. She stiffened and grasped him in a final, climactic surge of strength, coming just short of crushing Weatherbee's pelvis as she did so, and began to snuffle and sob with joy.

Lady Hawes went limp, and so did Weatherbee.

So far so good, he was thinking. Now came the hard part. Getting her the hell out of there so he could freshen up and dress again.

He sighed and gently kissed her thin lips. He could take another few moments here. It was only the polite and proper thing for a gentleman to do.

CHAPTER FIVE

Raider mouthed the dry grass stem and felt the tip of it crunch and crumble. At this time of year there was no sweet taste to the grass, no delicately flavored moisture inside it. Still, it made for awfully good grazing, cured into standing hay by the sun and dry winds of this semi-arid land. Beeves thrived on it. Raider nipped a quarter inch or so off the end that was in his mouth and spat it out on the ground in front of him. At his side Kenny did the same. Both of them were hunkered against the front wall of the soddy that served the new ranch as a barn. The chores had been done and now they were just waiting for Lucinda to come to the door and let them know she was done bathing and they could come inside again.

Raider picked up a bit of dried root that had fallen out of the sod wall and absently doodled in the dirt with it.

Kenny searched until he found a splinter and began to draw in the dirt as well.

Raider turned his head and pretended to cough so he could hide the smile that tugged at his lips. He wondered if the boy was aware of the imitation. Possibly not. No matter. The kid was learning. Already he could throw a rope as well as some grown men Raider knew, and that was after less than a week of practice. He had asked Raider to show him how just once, and ever since then the kid had spent nearly every spare moment of his time with a piece of busted hemp in his hands, teaching himself how to catch corral posts, buckets, whatever was handy. This afternoon he had managed to rope the family dog, which had pleased hell out of the kid if not the dog. Raider smiled again, remembering the delight of the one and the squirming of the other.

This visit seemed to be good for the kid, Raider concluded. Lucinda said so too.

Raider bit off another speck of grass stem, held it briefly on the tip of his tongue, and then spat. Beside him Kenny spat as well.

It had been—he had to think back for a bit to remember—a year and a half, maybe nearer two since Drew Latham shot John McCollum in the back. Yeah, Raider concluded. Closer to two years. Kenny hadn't been but nine then. He remembered his father well enough, but he hadn't learned all that much from him. He'd been too young. And McCollum hadn't had all that much time to spend with his son.

Raider sighed. McCollum had been a good man. Raider had not known him all that long, but he had liked him. They had worked well together, McCollum and Raider and Weatherbee. And then that son of a bitch Latham had got word that they were onto him and tried to solve his problem by eliminating the local law.

The SOB hadn't had as much luck getting rid of the Pinkertons, though. Raider had personally put a .44 slug into the bridge of Latham's nose. It hadn't brought John McCollum back to his family, but it was something.

And now, well, there was something kinda special about Lucinda McCollum. Raider hadn't expected this part of it to happen. Not exactly. But he was pleased that it had. Lucinda was one hell of a woman. Not as flashy as some he had known, but there was substance to her. It was comfortable just being with her. And with the kid, too, if the truth be told

Raider reached over and squeezed Kenny's shoulder. "You ma's done with her bath. You can get the bucket now."

"The door's still shut. How d'you figure she's ready for us to go in?" Kenny asked.

"The tub's to the right of the door. An' the mirror. Her wardrobe is to the left. I seen her shadow on the shade twice now, once going from the tub over to her bed an' again coming back. By now she's brushing out her hair. Another minute an' she'll be hollerin' for us to come inside."

"I didn't see that."

"A man's got to keep his eyes open, Kenny. Got to know what's going on around you, whether you think there's any reason or not. Good habit to have." Raider bit off another quarter inch of grass stem, mouthed it, and spat.

Kenny nodded solemnly at him and then jumped to his feet to fetch the milk bucket. There was no telling how long it had been since the boy had had milk on the table before Raider arrived, but it hadn't taken all that much for Raider to find a cow that had lost its calf and drive it inside the soddy so he could start the gentling process. Before he left, the cow should be calmed enough that the boy would be able to handle milking by himself. For the time being, Raider had to help control the mostly wild range cow.

As Raider expected, before Kenny could come back outside with the bucket of frothy, still warm milk, the door swung open, spilling a rectangle of yellow lamplight onto the ground between the house and barn. Lucinda stood there in her nightdress with the light behind her. Her figure was outlined in dark, shadowy curves against the backlighted cloth, and Raider felt a quick surge of desire for her that he hoped the boy did not notice.

"All done," Lucinda called.

"We're on our way." Raider stood upright and let the boy go ahead of him, lugging the heavy bucket and trying not to slosh any of the milk over the rim. A little bit spilled, and Kenny gave Raider a worried glance of apology.

"You're doin' okay," Raider encouraged. With a frown of concentration Kenny held the bucket out away from him with both hands so he wouldn't bump it against his leg again and carried it inside.

"Your turn next," Raider said when the bucket of milk was safely deposited on the kitchen table.

Kenny looked toward his mother and hesitated.

"Do what you're told, son."

Raider touched her elbow. "I don't think that's what he meant."

Lucinda raised an eyebrow.

"A man likes some privacy too, you know."

"But I've—"

Raider took her firmly by the arm and led her outside. The look Kenny gave him was proof enough that Raider had guessed correctly. The kid was feeling too grown up to be taking his bath with his ma in the same room.

Lucinda looked strangely sad as she walked with Raider toward the barn. "This is the first time...I mean, I've washed his back for him every—"

"Sure," Raider laughed, "an' his bottom, too. But that was when he was little. Now he figures he's most growed. Or hadn't you noticed?"

"Yes," Lucinda sighed. She linked her arm into Raider's and leaned against him as they walked. "But I suppose you're right." She smiled. "It makes me feel old. You know?"

Raider chuckled and slipped an arm around her slim waist. As soon as they were in the deep shadows inside the barn he turned her by the shoulders until they were belly to belly, then bent and kissed her.

Lucinda's arms wrapped around him and she pressed herself against him, deliberately rubbing the soft flat of her belly against his growing erection. Her mouth was soft and welcoming and good to taste.

"We shouldn't...get this started...till I've had a chance...at that tub...too." His efforts to form a coherent sentence were being interrupted by Lucinda's tongue. Not that he really minded much.

"Besides, what if...Kenny comes out here...before..."

"Shhh. He might think he's grown like you say, but I happen to know that he still likes to splash and play in the tub."

Lucinda stepped back away from him. She gathered the hem of her nightdress in her hands and with one fluid motion pulled the garment over her head and dropped it aside.

She stood there before him, silhouetted against the open barn door, her body tall and slim and proud. Her waist was small, her legs long and shapely, her neck and ankles delicate. Her breasts were not particularly large but certainly more than a mouthful, as he had proven to himself in the past and would again. They seemed exactly in the right proportion to the rest of her. Her stomach was just barely convex and delightfully soft over a scant patch of auburn hair.

Her hair, also a deep, rich auburn, unlike Kenny's carroty top, was long and hung in waves over her shoulders and down her back.

It was too dark inside the barn for him to see them now, but he well knew the sprinkling of freckles that dusted her shoulders and chest. Yet the flesh of her breasts was unblemished satin, delicately pink-tipped and very firm.

Her body was enough to make a man's mouth water. And Raider had reason to know that she was tighter and firmer than any woman with an eleven-year-old kid had any right to.

He reached for her, and Lucinda came into his arms again.

"Are you sure? I mean, I haven't got near that tub yet. I prob'ly smell bad and—"

"Hush." She closed his mouth by covering it with her own, and it was she who took his hand and drew him down onto the mound of wild grass hay that he and the boy had cut earlier.

She pulled him down on top of her, heedless of the sharp jut of his belt buckle and the buckle of his gunbelt, seeming to want his weight hard and demanding against her naked body.

She helped him fumble open his fly and arched her back to ease his entry.

She murmured with pleasure as he filled her, and whispered against his ear, "Later. When Kenny's asleep. You can get your bath then, dear. And you'll be clean, and I can take you into my mouth and taste you and feel the slick touch of you on my tongue." She shivered and moved her hips against him. "I'd like that, dear. If you would."

Raider's only answer was a low moan as the delicious feel and scents of Lucinda surrounded and overwhelmed him.

Slowly, very gently, he began to move inside her.

CHAPTER SIX

Weatherbee took a swallow of the chilled mineral water, cooled with slivers of cracked ice that had been cut last winter and stored in sawdust until now, then nodded a greeting to a couple who were strolling past. He recognized them, although he could not recall their names at the moment. In fact, he recognized nearly all of the people seated on the covered veranda of the mineral springs spa. There were not so many in attendance at this last gasp of the fashionable season. Last night's gala had been the final ball. From now until spring the only activity in Manitou would come from tubercular patients here for the dry atmosphere and the supposed healing qualities of the waters and baths from the natural springs. Nearly everyone within his view had been at the Antlers last night.

The woman, for instance, who was quite obviously heading toward a small table at the far side of the veranda. And who would perforce have to pass close by where Weatherbee sat with his chilled tonic water.

As she came nearer, Weatherbee stood and touched the brim of his silk hat.

"Miss von Hausen. I hope this lovely day finds you well." The remark and the polite smile that accompanied it were casual enough, certainly well within the bounds of propriety.

"Mr. Weatherbee. How do you do?" Emilie stopped by his table and extended a gloved hand toward him. He accepted it, barely touching her fingertips with his own.

Anyone watching—and a good many of those at the

other tables were sure to be—could never have guessed that Weatherbee had left this beautiful woman's rumpled bed only a matter of hours earlier.

Doc still had a pleasantly hollow ache deep in his groin from the pleasures the two of them had shared.

Emilie was, after all, the reason he had chosen to come here for his vacation.

"Would you care to join me, Miss von Hausen? Unless, of course, you have an engagement." The words meant nothing. They had agreed to meet at the spa before he slipped out of her room in the predawn and returned to his own.

"I would be delighted, Mr. Weatherbee." She mouthed the words with an actress's aplomb, but there was a sparkle in the bright china blue of her eyes that was meant for him alone. No onlooker could have interpreted that, even if anyone had been perceptive enough to notice.

Doc held a chair for her, and Emilie gracefully accepted his assistance. She laid her handbag and parasol aside and removed her gloves, folding them carefully and placing them on top of her bag.

A waiter was beside the table almost instantly, bowing, pencil poised over an unneeded notepad ready to take their order.

"Mineral water, Miss von Hausen?"

"Please. And a plate of croissants, I think."

Doc nodded to the waiter, confirming the order, and the man bowed swiftly away from the table.

Emilie chattered brightly about how simply devine the final gala had been, but, as before, what she was saying meant nothing. It was the look in her eyes that charmed Doc. The hidden meanings. She shifted position on the tiny chair and crossed her legs, contriving as she did so to bump the arch of one foot against Weatherbee's calf. Even if anyone had seen the contact, it would have seemed accidental. No one could possibly have noticed the split second of delay as her foot touched his leg, turning the "accidental" contact into a caress.

Doc was tempted to take her hand, however briefly, on whatever pretext. He glanced around to make sure no one was paying attention to them now that Emilie was seated.

Odd, he thought. There was a man seated alone on the far side of the serving area. The small table before him was bare, so he had not yet been served, yet he gave an impression of having been there for some time.

Doc tried to remember how long the fellow had been at that table, but he could not. Yet he had the impression that he had seen the man before. This morning? He didn't think so. Perhaps yesterday afternoon.

That was it. He had taken a stroll yesterday, from the Antlers down the hill to the railroad depot and then up again for a brisk walk through the town.

Of course. Weatherbee had stopped in at Perkins-Shearer to replace a necktie that was becoming frayed, and this same man—he was almost sure of it—had been standing outside admiring a display in the front windows of the store.

Odd coincidence, that, Doc thought.

The waiter brought Emilie's mineral water and a small plate of lemon wedges with it. Weatherbee offered her the lemon and, when she nodded, squeezed a wedge into the sparkling water for her.

He looked across the floor again, but now the fellow was gone.

Probably got tired of having to wait for service and left in a huff, Doc thought, when the lady was served before him.

Still and all, the cheeky fellow ought not to have been surprised. Miss von Hausen was most obviously a lady of quality, while the man had been average at best. Threadbare as his suit had been, it was almost a wonder he was admitted entrance in the first place.

Doc caught the look Emilie gave him with her smile and correct thank-you, and all thoughts of the out-of-place little man were wiped from his mind.

At this point he was thinking only of Emilie von Hausen and her unspoken promises about tonight.

CHAPTER SEVEN

"How d'you know there's a cow missing?" Kenny asked, reining his scruffy little pony closer to Raider's tall horse.

"Two reasons," Raider answered him, his eyes continuing to sweep the dense brush in the draw below where they rode. "One, your ma says the count is one short. Which is good enough. Also because I remember seeing this one before we started the gather, an' we didn't work her or her calf."

"But how could you know *which* cow?" Kenny insisted. The boy was not comfortable in the saddle, or at least did not look like he could be. He sat it awkwardly, stiffly, not flowing easily with the movement of the horse. But he was starting to learn. Time would take care of the rest of it.

And he was beginning to look like a ranch kid too. Until Raider's visit the boy had been forced to wear a battered straw hat and mostly went barefoot. Raider brought him a surplus but new Kossuth hat that made him look almost right on the back of the coarse little pony. Raider smiled to himself. He and the kid had spent most of an entire evening steaming the hatbrim into an acceptable shape and stuffing the band with scraps of cloth to make the thing fit right. Now the "grown-up" hat was Kenny's prized possession. Next, that is, to the pony.

"I remember the cow," Raider insisted. "Mind now, I told you a man has to pay attention to what's going on around him?"

Kenny nodded.

"Then you wait an' see if I'm not right. The one we're

looking for is dark colored, more liver than red. She has a broken tip on her right horn and a white patch under her jaw on the other side." Raider smiled at him. "An' she'll have a calf with her."

"How would you know that? You seen it, too?"

"Nope. Or not to know it, anyhow. She was with some others cows when I seen her, and there was several calves mixed in amongst them."

"Then how would you know?"

"Think about it for a bit." Raider kneed his horse down from the ridgetop they had been following so he could get a better look into a particularly dense and nasty piece of brush in the bottom below. He saw nothing down there but the flutter of a bird's wings and returned to the ridge. If they had been hunting men instead of cattle, or if this was country where he might have expected danger, he would have done things differently. But he was trying to teach Kenny the business of working cattle, not chasing men. Here he had no need to avoid skylining himself.

Kenny rode silently at his side for several minutes. Then the kid's face broadened into a huge grin of comprehension. "You seen she had a full bag, right?"

"Exactly." Raider made the one word sound like a high compliment.

"An' you'd remember all that?"

"You will too when you get the hang of it."

"Boy, I don' know."

"You will," Raider assured him.

The country here was broken and dry, hot even at this late time of year. But in the bottoms where water pooled beneath the surface the grass was thick and rich. It was good land for a stockman. A land full of hope and promise. A wide, free land where a man—or a widowed woman with determination—could build for the future, and a place where a boy could grow into all the manhood he wanted to handle. Raider glanced down toward the kid who was riding so close beside him. The tall, jet-haired Pinkerton operative smiled while the boy was looking elsewhere. Yeah, this was a pretty damn good way to spend a vacation. Better than he had expected even.

"Bull calf or heifer?" Kenny asked.

"Now how the hell would I know that?"

The kid grinned. He had known the answer to that one before he asked the question. He had gotten one over on Raider.

"All right, smart aleck," Raider said. "The calf's a heifer."

"Now how . . . ?"

"Wait and see," was all Raider would tell him. The truth, of course, was that Raider had no way in the world to tell what the calf would be. But he had a fifty-fifty chance of being right. If he was right, the kid would be impressed as hell. If Raider was wrong, it would give the boy the satisfaction of catching his idol out in a mistake. No harm done either way.

"Look sharp now. I c'n smell cow down there." Raider stood in his stirrups and flared his nostrils. Then shook his head. "Nope. Can't tell yet how fresh. Sure do smell somethin', though."

Kenny gave him a skeptical look, then turned and began to look more closely into the screen of thick brush in the bottom of the draw.

In fact, Raider had already spotted the movement of pale hide low to the ground. The half-seen motion had been too brief for him to tell for sure if he had seen the swish of a bedded deer's tail or the shift of a cow's hock. But he had definitely seen something. He did not tell the boy that. Better to let Kenny make the discovery if he could.

The animal moved again as the two riders came closer. This time Kenny spotted it too.

"Look." He pointed.

"Where?" Raider leaned closer to him, pretending not to see the cow and calf that were tensed, ready to run from the far side of the small thicket.

"There." Kenny sounded excited. He pointed again.

"By damn, you're right."

The boy rewarded Raider with a beam of pure pleasure. *He* had been the one to spot them.

"Good, Kenny."

The boy's grin became bigger.

Raider reined his horse to a halt and leaned down to whisper to the kid. "We don't want to spook them now. If we bust straight down on them they'll run the wrong way. We want to haze them back toward the pen, right?"

Kenny nodded solemnly.

"I want you to ride down off the ridge, over there where they won't be able to see you, down about a half mile. Then drift real slow up this way. Mind you come on slow, an' keep on the far side o' the bottom so they'll come out on this side, which is where we want 'em."

"Which one will you rope when they come out?" Kenny asked. He was obviously thinking it would be easier to drag the calf than the cow. And probably thinking too that he would be able to handle the calf if that was the one Raider wanted roped.

Raider chuckled. "Not neither of 'em for a while. Hell, kid, it's five, maybe six miles back to the house. We don't wanta try and drag anything all that ways. We'll just hang back and drift 'em slow and easy the way we want 'em to go. Okay?"

The boy seemed mildly disappointed. He was itching to try his roping skills. Raider made a mental note to let Kenny rope the calf once they had calf and mama inside the pen. It could do no harm then and would be good for the boy.

"Go on now."

Kenny turned his pony, taking it practically under the neck of Raider's mount to get to the side of the ridge away from the suspicious cow below. As soon as he thought he was safely out of the cow's line of sight he thumped the round, tubby barrel of the shaggy pony and forced the reluctant animal into a lope, doing exactly as Raider had told him.

Raider smiled to himself as he watched the kid, so earnest and eager about this simple task.

Next time he got the chance, Raider thought, he would have to see if he could find the boy a pair of spurs. And maybe some cheap boots, too, by damn, instead of those clodhopper shoes Lucinda insisted on putting him in.

Raider blinked. Suddenly amused with himself. Why, hell, here he was thinking about spending his plunder on a damned eleven-year-old kid. And wasn't *that* a change of pace. Usually a dollar in his pocket meant just that much foofaraw he could buy to entice a good-timing girl. And here he was planning to spend some of it instead on a skinny boy with a carrot top and freckles. What the hell was going on with him lately?

He shrugged to himself, deliberately unwilling to dredge up the ancient and unpleasant memories of his own boyhood at that same age. Piss on it, he told himself firmly. If he wanted to do it, it was nobody's damned business but his own. Fuck anybody that wanted to say different. He eased back in the saddle, reins loose, and let the horse drop its head a bit as he hooked a knee over his saddle horn and waited for the boy to get into position. The bright late morning sun felt warm and pleasant on his back, and tonight there would be the boy's ma to help take out any kinks in his spine. Yeah, Raider thought, this was all right.

He looked down toward where the cow, accepting his presence better now that she had seen no threatening moves from him and was not being crowded, nuzzled her calf's butt as it moved under her flank and began to nurse.

Ever vigilant, Raider's eyes left the cow, flicked briefly down toward Kenny, who was still loping south before he made his move over the ridge and into the lower end of the bottom, then up again to sweep the horizon.

He frowned.

He could almost have sworn he'd caught a flash of sunlight on metal somewhere over on that next ridge. But the flash—if indeed he had seen something flash—had been barely perceptible out of the corner of his eye. And it was gone now, if in fact he had really seen it.

He shrugged again. Likely he had been wrong. Or if he had seen anything, well, likely it was just the sun glinting off a speck of mica in an exposed rock. Something like that.

Likely it was no more than that.

Still, for no reason he could have explained to the boy,

Raider felt a sudden chill race up his spine. And he had this half-conscious sense that he was being watched.

Funny that he hadn't felt anything like that before.

He stood in his stirrups and stared in that direction. But he saw nothing.

Down below Kenny had crossed the ridge and was coming up the bottom now at a slow, careful walk. The cow raised her head and looked in the boy's direction, forgetting about Raider for the moment. As the boy and pony came slowly within a quarter mile of her, she nudged her calf off her bag and turned, moving into full view on the near side of the thicket and then leading the calf—it was a bull calf, Raider could see now—in the direction they wanted.

Raider forgot his momentary sense of unease and quietly turned his horse into position, reminding the cow that he was there, and therefore influencing the direction she would take.

Kenny was doing just fine, Raider observed. With luck they should have the cow and calf penned in time so that they could eat their lunch at the house today. Which would please Raider well enough, although he suspected that Kenny was still thinking of their half-cooked range meals as a treat rather than a burden.

The cow veered away from the desired path, and Raider made a very slight adjustment in the direction his horse was taking, quietly and subtly influencing the cow and calf back onto the line the man wanted them to take. It was slow, patient work, with neither Raider nor the boy making any attempt to come close to the cow, instead hanging back a good four hundred yards or more and guiding her so carefully that the cow probably didn't realize she was being driven. Raider would not make any attempt to force her until they neared the pen. Then, but only then, the riding would be fast and furious. And probably would please the hell out of the kid. Meantime, though, Raider was going to teach him the right way to handle this.

By then he had completely forgotten that moment of uneasiness when he thought someone was watching him. By then he had other things to think about.

CHAPTER EIGHT

There was that man again.

Doc was sure of it this time. He had been there yesterday at the spa. Weatherbee was almost sure it was the same man who had been behind that high-held newspaper in the hotel lobby last night.

And now there he was again on the far side of the dining room when Doc came down for breakfast.

It all could be a coincidence, of course. The fellow could simply be another guest registered at the Antlers. If so it would be only reasonable for them to run into each other frequently.

Of course, he did not look like a gentleman who would be staying at a fine hotel.

On the other hand, he could simply be eccentric. Perhaps he had made his bundle in mining. A good number of the old-time prospectors who became suddenly rich remained stubbornly odd in their clothing and other habits. And *very* few business establishments were so determined about their standards that they would turn away a man who was wealthy, regardless of the gentleman's personal habits.

It was possible, Doc conceded to himself, but unlikely. Truly unlikely. Surely one of the socially conscious snobs —and Doc had to concede that many of his fellow guests here, including Donald Lampkin, fell into that category— would have pointed the fellow out if he were really a rich eccentric.

The waiter came with the breakfast Doc had ordered— cold quail with toast and shirred eggs. Doc pondered the likelihood of coincidences while he ate.

Better, he decided, to find out than to wonder. It should be easily done.

He glanced again across the room toward the man, pretending to smile and wave at a passing couple so the fellow would not be onto him.

The man was dressed very much as he had been yesterday, in the same cuff-frayed suit, and quite possibly in the same limp-collared shirt as well.

It was his footwear Doc was mostly interested in, though. The couple Doc had waved to, the Harbitons, passed on by, and Doc could see beneath the cloth on the man's table. The fellow was wearing ordinary shoes, stockings without spats. Doc grunted to himself. If the fellow was really following him...

Weatherbee ate quickly and signed the chit with his name and room number, then hurried upstairs to change out of the suit he had chosen for the day.

When he came downstairs again he was dressed in tweeds—coat, vest, and knickerbocker-length hiking trousers. He had exchanged his derby for an Irish tweed walking cap. Most important, he was now wearing tall, lace-up logging boots with long woolen stocking rolled down over the boot tops. He was carrying his oldest and stoutest walking stick.

"Off to the Garden, Weatherbee?" Lampkin asked in passing. The man added a wink and said, "You should've been with us yesterday, old chap."

"Yes. Pity I couldn't," Doc lied. He paused to exchange a few comments with Lampkin. While he did so he looked for the little man. There was no sign of the fellow now. Perhaps Doc was mistaken. Perhaps it was simply coincidence. Doc excused himself from the conversation and left the hotel.

He walked down to the rail depot, still without spotting the man he suspected was shadowing him, and paid his quarter for the short run to Manitou. If the man was actually tailing him, he was doing an unexpectedly good job of it. Doc did not see him on the cars.

The narrow-gauge train pulled into Manitou after a mere

fifteen-minute journey, and Weatherbee disembarked with the other late-season holiday passengers.

Most of the people who had been on the train turned toward the spa, but Doc hiked purposefully up Ruxton toward the start of the Barr Trail. The trail wound its slow path up onto the top of Pikes Peak, either by foot for the vigorous or by mule for those who preferred to ride in exchange for a fee.

Doc dawdled along deliberately, giving the little man plenty of time to find and follow if he wished. When he reached the foot of the trail, Weatherbee stopped near the mule barn to light an Old Virginia. He leaned against a corral rail and watched with amusement as a group of young women, probably clinging to the final days of their first season as eligible debutantes, were settled with more or less comfort into the sidesaddles on the mules they would ride to the peak.

The hostlers seemed not at all awed by the wealth or the beauty of the girls, teasing them repeatedly and winking at one another behind the girls' backs. For the most part the young men were lean, rugged-looking boys of college age but without the means, or possibly the inclination, to pursue higher education. They were, though, obviously interested in other pursuits. And Doc had to admit that employment here gave them more than ample opportunity to admire the shape of a young lady's ankle.

The mule train was assembled, a guide was assigned for their safety, and the bevy of chattering young ladies filed up onto the trail. Doc let them get well ahead before he extinguished the stub of his cheroot and started up afoot after them. There still had been no sign of the odd little man.

Weatherbee hiked up the trail at a swift, steady pace for the better part of half an hour. He did not mind the excursion. In fact, he was thoroughly enjoying it. There was a crisp, invigorating smell of impending fall in the thin air, and in just the past few days the aspens along the lower end of the trail had begun to turn color.

Higher up, the mountainsides looked like they had been sheathed in pure gold from the brilliant colors. Closer by, a few stands of shrub oak were a burnished red and copper hue. It was a fine time of year.

Doc checked his watch, decided he had gone far enough for the moment, and looked about for a suitable stopping point.

He found a slab of flat red rock, brushed it off, and took a seat. He was in no hurry now. He pulled another cheroot from his coat pocket, lighted it, and settled down to wait and to watch.

The stub of that cheroot had long since grown cold and he was smoking another when finally he heard the rattle of hooves climbing toward him on the stony trail. A young couple, probably newlyweds, had passed him on foot, but it was the next mule train that interested him.

Dressed as he had been, the too frequently visible stranger could not possibly have hoped to pass himself off as a hiker. So if he was going to follow Weatherbee up the trail he would almost certainly have to do it in a mule party.

The guide, bored and riding easily in the saddle of his undersized mule, came into view around the last curve below where Doc waited, then one by one the dudes he was guiding.

There was a middle-aged woman, a teenaged girl, a lad of twelve or so, a man who was almost certainly the father of the two youngsters, a pair of young women, a young gentleman who seemed to be accompanying them, and— Doc smiled inwardly—a smallish man whom Doc recognized quite well by now.

In his suit and low shoes the man seemed out of place, but not so much so as if he had been hiking.

Weatherbee turned away from the approaching mule train and pretended to be absorbed in making an adjustment to the tightness of his boot laces. He waved casually when the group went by him. The little man who was riding at the rear of the train appeared not to pay any attention to him.

But Doc knew better.

He waited until the group was out of sight, then he openly smiled.

The poor man, whoever he was and whatever he wanted, was committed to the journey now. Unless he was willing to make himself obvious about it, he would have to go all the way to the top with the mules.

Still smiling, and not at all concerned, Weatherbee retied his boot laces, picked up his walking stick, and started back down the trail. Toward Manitou.

While the man who was supposed to be following him was steadily climbing in the opposite direction.

CHAPTER NINE

Raider rode into the ranch yard and dismounted. He could see the top of Lucinda's auburn-hued head bobbing behind the scantling fence he had built to contain the two dozen young chicks she had bought. His personal opinion was that the stupid birds would not make it, what with coyotes and hawks and bobcats and who knew what other kinds of predators anxious to make a meal off them. But Lucinda was sure she could raise the creatures here, and he had to admit that they would be a fine addition to the livestock if she could somehow get them through to laying age.

He tied his horse to the rail he had erected in front of the barn and slapped the dust from his britches. Lucinda must have heard him. A moment later the chicken pen gate opened and she looked out.

Alarm crossed her face when she saw that Raider was alone, and she came rushing toward him. "Where's Kenny?"

"Whoa. It's okay." Raider grinned at her. "You know that hole where the cattle water when the creek's running?"

She shook her head.

"That ain't important, I guess. Anyway, the point is, that spot could hold water most o' the year if it's dug out and improved a bit. Him and me poked around enough to know there's water in the creekbed three, four feet down."

"Yes?"

Raider grinned again. "So I gave the kid a shovel an' told him to build himself a water hole. He'll be at it till dark." He slipped an arm around her waist and pulled her close.

"That's terrible," she accused.

"Naw. Good for 'im." He winked. "And for you and me."

"*You're* terrible." Lucinda poked him in the ribs.

"Ouch! Damn it, that hurt." He pulled away from her and went into the barn, where he began searching through a jumble of tools leaning in a corner.

"What are you doing now?" she demanded.

"Lookin' for a shovel. If I'm so terrible, I reckon I ought to be out there with the kid makin' myself useful."

"I didn't say you were *that* terrible."

When he turned to look she was standing at the barn entrance with her blouse unbuttoned and hanging loose. She shrugged it off her shoulders and tossed it aside. She kicked off her heavy work shoes and slid her skirt down over ripe-swelling hips.

Raider whistled appreciatively.

Lucinda smiled and turned, posing for him, hands on hips and head canted to the side. Twisting and turning in the sunlight so that he could admire the sleek curves and planes of her figure.

Raider's mouth felt dry. He licked his lips. And reached for this woman who excited him beyond all reason. She melted to him, raised her face to his with her mouth open and lips eagerly searching for his. He could feel the heat of her through his clothing. He could feel her need, matching his own, as she opened herself to him.

Within seconds his clothing had been thrown aside and they lay locked together on the hay pile.

Later Lucinda sat up. She lifted her hands to fuss with her hair. Her neat, tidy bun had become quite mused during the last few minutes. She tried to put things right again, but it was a losing battle. After a moment she gave up, pulling the pins that had held it and letting her hair fall in a dark, rich spill down the milky softness of her shoulders and back. Raider was sorry she had quit. The lift of her arms had done marvelously interesting things to her breasts. Idly he picked up a hay stem and began to chew on it while Lucinda lay back into the crook of his arm. She felt good there. Right and natural. He had just taken her, and already he wanted this woman again.

Perhaps—the thought startled him—perhaps for many days to come. Even for *all* his days to come.

Never had Raider felt this way about anyone before. But he did about Lucinda. And, he admitted to himself, he could damn well enjoy having the kid around too. Kenny's uncontained admiration of the tall, black-haired Pinkerton operative was one helluva compliment. Between the boy and his mother they made him feel... good. They did, damn it. He was not used to this kind of feeling. He certainly was not accustomed to this sense of family closeness. It was something he had never known in his boyhood. He had observed it in others, of course, but he had never known it himself. Not really.

And now... Now, by damn, he kinda liked it.

Not just kind of, either. He *did* like it. Plenty.

He pulled Lucinda closer, enjoying the quietly comfortable feel of her against him as she pressed her face against his neck with a sigh.

Raider shook his head in silent wonder. He simply could not believe the pleasures this woman gave him. And not just in the sack, either. He was used to that. No, what he was finding here included that but went far beyond. Into something better. Something he had never really known before.

He turned his head to the side, so that he could look out into the bright glare of the afternoon sunlight.

It wasn't bad country out there. Not spectacular like the mountains to the north. And not the richness of the big-grass country up on the high plains. This land was something else again. In a way like the McCollum family. Quietly pleasing.

To his own surprise he found himself wondering if he could be content staying on this land. Away from the excitement of movement and manhunt, new faces and new places and always some hell to raise.

By damn, he was really thinking about it.

He could hardly believe that. But he was.

And the prospect... why, it was pretty nice, now that he thought on it some.

Almost exciting in its own kind of way.

He looked past the house, to the rolling, mostly arid land beyond.

Raider chuckled softly to himself. He had sworn, by God, that he wouldn't ever walk behind a plow again. He'd had a bellyful of that shit, with that son of a bitch of an old man of his always pushing and prodding and bitching for more, no matter how much work a body got in from sunup to sungo.

No, he'd had a plenty of that.

But a man could run cattle without having to push a damn plow, couldn't he? Hell yes, he could. Maybe have to swing a scythe now and then to get some hay laid by. But that wasn't the same thing. It wasn't like plowing. A man could handle a scythe and still keep his pride. Hell yes, he could.

Raider felt the rhythm of Lucinda's breathing slow and subtly alter. She had drifted off into a light sleep. He smiled. And there was this sense of warmth, protectiveness he guessed it was, that he felt toward her when he knew she was sleeping gentle and content in his arms.

Damn! He really could not believe the things he was thinking and feeling just now.

Scared him in a way. But excited him too.

Lucinda right there with him. And Kenny, too. The kid had a lot to learn, but he wasn't any shirker. All he needed was to be taught, told what to do and showed just one time how to do it. Raider was kinda enjoying doing that showing. It was all the kind of thing that John would have shown his son if he'd been alive to do it. But John McCollum wasn't there anymore, and every kid needs a pa, even if the pa hasn't exactly had all that much experience at that particular job.

Raider blinked with surprise at the thought of being a pa, even a secondhand one.

And, hell, there wasn't any reason, none that he knew

of, why him and Lucinda couldn't maybe have a kid of their own someday too.

Raider found himself wondering if a kid like that would have Kenny's red hair or if it would have Raider's jet coloring.

Hell, maybe it would be a girl. With that dark, gleaming auburn that looked so good on Lucinda.

Raider could stand that thought. A pretty little girl with her hair done up in ribbons. He snorted angrily at the thought of the pimple-faced little sons of bitches that would be panting around any girl as pretty as Lucinda was. Well, Raider knew a thing or two about *that*. The little bastards would have to watch their step, or Raider would be there to snap assholes with them. He would for a fact.

Lordy, but this line of thinking was taking him to strange places.

His snort of imagined anger roused Lucinda. She stirred and moved in his arms, then sat sleepily upright and began to fuss with her hair again. She yawned and blinked, then moved away from him.

"Where're you going?"

"I should start supper cooking or we'll have to have it for breakfast instead."

"I've been thinking that we'll be needing some fresh meat," Raider said, sitting up beside her. "Besides, it's about time the boy learned how to hunt."

"Do you think he should learn so soon? He's only eleven. That's too young to handle a gun."

Raider grunted. "He's big enough to pick one up. That means he's big enough to handle one. Besides, Kenny's smart. 'Bout as smart a kid as I've ever seen."

Lucinda seemed more pleased by that than if he had paid her a compliment.

"If you think so," she said, deferring to his judgment. She brushed some loose hay off her shoulder and turned her back so Raider could brush there where she could not reach. He didn't at all mind performing the chore, and his hand lingered on her flesh longer than was necessary.

"None of that now," she warned. "I have to get the

stove going." She softened the refusal with a wink and a promise. "Later, dear."

He grinned at her wickedly, stood and helped her to her feet, then turned her around so he could brush her backside with more long, lingering strokes of his palm.

"Later," she said. She sounded exasperated, and this time he was not sure if she was joking or not. He left her alone and began pulling his clothing back on. Lucinda was also dressing.

"If you're going to teach Kenny to hunt," she said idly, "you should have started this afternoon."

"What d'you mean?"

"When you chased those little deer out of the thicket."

He raised an eyebrow in her direction. He had no idea what in hell she was getting at.

"You know. Out of the thicket over there." She pointed off toward the northwest. "I saw you boys ride down close to it, and two whitetail jumped out the other side of it." She sighed. "They're so pretty I almost hate to eat them, you know?"

"I still don't know what deer you're talking about," Raider insisted.

"You know. Just after lunch. Right over there."

Raider felt a chill of concern.

"Lucinda, honey, me and Kenny weren't anywhere near that thicket just after lunch. We rode straight over to the creekbed an' that water hole Kenny's working on."

"But I saw..." she started to insist. She shook her head abruptly, but Raider could see the worry in her eyes.

*Some*one had been there. And it wasn't Raider or Kenny she had seen riding down toward that thicket.

CHAPTER TEN

Weatherbee's shadow was back on duty the following morning. The only real difference now was that the little man was making no effort to keep himself hidden from Doc's observation. He obviously realized now that he had been spotted. But instead of giving up the game, whatever it was, he chose to linger in and near the hotel, keeping a perfectly obvious watch on Doc's movements.

It was damnably annoying, Doc thought. Particularly since today he had made arrangements to "accidentally" run into Emilie during a tour of the Garden of the Gods.

Emilie von Hausen was a woman of rare if hidden passions, and she had expressed a desire to quench those passions in the open air, surrounded by the beauties of nature.

Doc had been able to think of no place on earth that would have been more appropriate for such a diversion than the Garden, with its towers and spires and massifs of wind- and water-carved bright red sandstone.

And, almost as important, with its very few visitors at this late season.

The idea had been for each of them, separately, to take one of the tourist omnibuses that conducted visitors through the parklike Garden, Emilie direct from the Antlers, Weatherbee by way of the spa at nearby Manitou.

They were to meet at lunchtime and slip away for some private pursuits high on one of the great formations of rock. Doc had been there before. The spot he had in mind was isolated from any ground-level view but completely open to the sky, with truly spectacular vistas of the mountains toward the west and the sweep of the distant grasslands to the east. Better yet, the walk to the summit of the formation was as easy as a Sunday stroll if one only knew the correct route to take, although from any vantage point or trail normally followed by visitors the formation appeared to be an unclimbable crag.

It was perfect. Except, of course, for that damned man who was watching Weatherbee so diligently.

Doc frowned and wondered if he could give the fellow the slip again.

Yesterday's deception had only been intended to verify that the man was indeed deliberately observing Doc. The fact that it had also put the fellow off the scent for a few hours was quite incidental.

Now, damn it, the man was alerted. He would be more careful. And it would be easier for him, since he was no longer trying to hide himself from his quarry.

Damn the cheeky fellow anyway.

Doc wondered—as he had been steadily for much of the early morning—who this man was and why he was spying on a vacationing Pinkerton operative.

The only thing Doc could conclude was that the man was not so much interested in an operative named Weatherbee as he was, perhaps, interested in Emilie von Hausen and her possible admirers.

Emilie had told him herself, with unexpected candor, that she was being courted by a gentleman from Washington—she refrained from being specific about the identity of the gentleman yet gave an impression that he was wealthy, powerful, and quite probably involved in a high level of government service—who was excessively jealous of her attentions.

It was possible, Doc concluded, that the spy was trying to determine if Weatherbee was here to see Miss von Hausen. As of course he was, damn it.

It would serve no one good if the two of them were caught in an assignation, regardless of the reasons behind the spying.

Emilie had a reputation to protect. Weatherbee had his own good name to concern him—his and of course his family's. He had caused his family quite enough embarrassment by his choice of career. They did not deserve scandal on top of all that.

He sighed and wondered reluctantly if he should simply fail to arrive at the picnic luncheon today. Emilie would be angry, but surely she would see the wisdom of discretion in the matter.

It was she, after all, whom Weatherbee was trying to protect.

Emilie had as good as told him that she was giving serious thought to accepting the Washington gentleman's proposal.

This trip west might well turn out to be her last fling of freedom before she accepted the benefits—and the restrictions—of a wedded life.

Doc would hardly want to ruin that possibility for her—in part, he had to admit to himself, because any disruption of her planning at this point would be at least partially his fault. And as much as he enjoyed their private moments together—and he certainly did—his intentions toward the lady were transitory at best.

He enjoyed bedding her quite as much as she enjoyed —insisted upon—being bedded. But the wedded life was not for him. Not with this woman or any other, at least as far as his current expectations allowed. He acknowledged to himself that this might someday change, but he was in no hurry for a life of permanent boredom. Not even the delightful Emilie could sway his thinking on that subject. If there was a woman who could or would make him think differently, Weatherbee had not yet met her.

He sighed again. Thoughts about that were doing nothing to resolve his current problem, which was the planned afternoon delight and the possible inclusion of a third party to the tryst.

Damn the fellow anyway.

Doc pulled his watch from his vest pocket and checked the time. The trains to Manitou ran too frequently for that to be of concern, but the coach to the Garden would leave the spa promptly at eleven. It was now half past nine, and it would take the better part of half an hour to reach the spa from the hotel. That left him very little time to lose his unwanted companion.

Then he grunted softly to himself. Subtlety seemed unnecessary now that the fellow knew Doc was aware of him. That was something.

Doc set aside the newspaper he had not been able to focus on since breakfast and walked quickly out of the lobby of the elegant hotel. The little man folded his own paper, tucked it under his arm, and hurried out into the sunshine behind Weatherbee.

Doc turned left on Cascade and walked quickly uptown. He passed the first block of storefronts, turned right on Bijou, then left again on Tejon. The little man was close behind.

Weatherbee went past a storefront, stopped, and quickly doubled back—a transparent attempt to shake his follower—and hurried out the back door into an alley.

The little man disappeared behind him, which Doc did not for a moment believe. The fellow was playing possum with him—exactly what Doc would have done himself if their roles had been reversed. Weatherbee was, after all, no stranger to the art of tailing a suspect.

Doc hurried down the alley, turned left and then right again, so that he was walking quickly north on Cascade once more.

There was still no sign of the spy behind him, but that meant nothing except that the fellow wanted Doc to believe that he had gotten away with the simple trick.

He continued beyond the downtown district, onto the shaded residential avenues that lay to the north of the city. Here it was more difficult for the little man to avoid being spotted. He was still back there, several blocks away and doing a rather good job of not being seen. Doc pretended not to know he was there and hurried on at a quick clip.

He held that pace nearly to the outskirts of the town, then turned left again, crossed Wood, and broke into a run, down away from the building plots to the tangled brush that lined the creekbank.

From here it was a simple footrace to the livery that Doc remembered on the eastern edge of Colorado City.

And Doc had no doubt whatsoever about which of the two of them was in the better physical condition.

Just let the silly shadow try and stay with him now. And with any degree of luck at all, he would still be in plenty of time to rent a horse and reach the picnic grounds in time to meet Emilie there.

Alone, thank goodness.

But he realized with a sense of sadness that this might well be the last time he would be able to meet Emilie in private. He did, though, have to see her so he could explain the situation to her and warn her that her gentleman friend might be having her watched.

That was something of a pity.

He laughed softly to himself as he loped swiftly through the brush. If he got hard up he could always arrange another private meeting with Lady Hawes.

CHAPTER ELEVEN

Raider went to the door and stepped outside. Behind him Lucinda and Kenny were busy washing the supper dishes, Lucinda washing and Kenny drying. The boy's mouth was going a mile a minute, yakking about everything he and Raider had done today. This dishwashing time seemed to be their time to talk, and Raider did not want to intrude on it.

Besides, he was becoming worried. More and more worried as he thought about it.

Day before yesterday there had been those riders Lucinda mistook for him and Kenny down by the thicket.

Then yesterday more glinting reflections of sun striking metal or glass.

And now today Raider had seen the riders himself, a couple of different times and in a couple of different directions. Enough times and enough places to make him think that maybe there were more than just the two men Lucinda had seen.

And too close to the house for comfort.

It would have been different if the men, whoever they were, had come in to ask for water or a meal or something. Or just to announce themselves as being in the area on some kind of honest business.

But they hadn't. Whoever they were, they just hung out there at a distance. Seeming to watch. Seeming to want to come no closer, yet making no real effort to hide themselves.

Raider couldn't figure it out. And what he could not

understand, whatever seemed unnatural, was suspicious, possibly even threatening.

For the first time in days he was conscious of the big Remington that rode at his waist. Except for a routine cleaning now and then he had not handled the revolver, or really thought about it, since he arrived. He had even been thinking that maybe he would be more comfortable working the McCollum cattle if he started carrying the Remington in his saddlebags while he was here. A stockman might occasionally need the use of a rifle to dispatch a coyote, but handguns were generally considered town wear, the drawings in *Harper's Weekly* and the *Police Gazette* notwithstanding.

Now he was glad he had the weapon handy.

He walked out into the cool night air and gave his eyes time to adjust, then hiked up the nearest rise so he could get a better look around.

Below, the yellow lamplight coming through the cabin windows looked warm and inviting. Inviting to whom? Raider had to wonder.

Were the men out there planning harm to a woman they might have heard was alone out here with just a kid for protection?

It could be. A man never knew. And surely people would have paid attention to any woman as pretty as Lucinda when she made her infrequent trips to town.

Raider bridled at the thought of someone doing her hurt.

Whoever was out there, they were not neighbors.

The only neighbors close enough to have legitimate business on this stretch of grass were a graying, dried-up couple who had taken up land fourteen, fifteen miles south. But Raider had met them. They knew he was visiting. They would not have hesitated to swing by to deliver a howdy if it was they he had seen. Certainly they would have stopped in for coffee if they had been as close to the house as those riders Lucinda had seen down by the thicket.

So it was somebody else out there. And Raider was getting angry as he thought about it.

It was looking more and more like the riders could be someone who wanted to do Lucinda hurt. That he would not allow.

He grunted to himself as he hiked the last few yards to the top of the rise and stood surveying the countryside in all directions.

There, by damn. Off to the northeast, a mile or better, he could see the faint flicker of a campfire.

Now why in hell would any honest person want to stay out like that when he could ride in and be sure of a hot meal and a place to spread his bedroll. No reason that Raider could think of.

Raider stood for a moment glaring toward the firelight.

Indecision was not his way, though. Neither was inaction.

Whoever the bastards were, he was going to face them.

Whatever it was they wanted around here, they could name their game up front and out loud.

Or damn well answer to him about it.

He wheeled and started down the slope toward the barn and his waiting horse.

He thought about telling Lucinda and the boy where he was going. But that would only alarm them. Better for him to take care of this without causing them concern, he decided as he saddled the horse, picked up his Winchester, and swung onto the animal.

Likely he would be back before they even knew he was gone. It always took them longer than was necessary to wash the supper dishes. They spent a helluva lot more time talking than they did working. So it should be all right for him to slip away and take care of this, whatever it was, and just be back and the whole thing over with before they knew he was gone.

Yeah, he thought. That would be the right thing to do.

He guided the horse slowly away from the house so they would not be apt to hear him leaving, then bumped the animal into an easy canter over the familiar ground.

Up ahead he could see the beacon of the campfire. It would take him only ten minutes or so to ride over there, ten or so more to come back.

Sure, he could be back before Lucinda and the boy had to worry about anything.

Raider rode with the chill night air in his face, never once thinking that by leaving he might have placed the defenseless woman and boy in danger behind him.

CHAPTER TWELVE

The ride was actually something of a pleasure. If he hadn't been worried about the men who had no apparent business here Raider would have enjoyed it. The night air felt clean and crisp in his lungs, and the horse moved fluidly and well beneath him. Any other night he would have thought a moonlight run like this a lark. And in fact he was already thinking that some evening very soon when Kenny was settled in with his studies—there was no time for them during the day, and Lucinda insisted that he keep on plugging at them—perhaps Raider and Lucinda could ride together for the evening. Possibly all the way over to the creekbed, where there was a stand of soft, sweet grass that he knew about.

That would be for a someday thing, though. Now he had serious business to attend to.

He rode directly toward the dim gleam of the firelight, making no attempt to hide his coming or to muffle the sound of the horse's hoofs. Whoever these men were they just might have a legitimate reason to be here. He didn't want to start trouble by accident, coming at them unexpected out of the dark. On the other hand, if it was trouble they did want . . .

He hefted the Winchester in his hand, felt of the familiar balance of the steel and wood. The weapon was not slung under his leg tonight, and the Remington was free in the holster on his belt. Just in case.

The fire seemed to appear no larger as he came closer to it. It was dying even as he rode toward it. No one had replenished the quickly burned fuel recently, so possibly the men around it had already rolled in for the night.

Which would explain why he didn't see any movement between himself and the dancing, dimming flames.

Raider called out a polite hello as he came close to the camp, stopped the horse outside the small ring of light thrown by the low fire, and dismounted, Winchester still in hand.

No one moved in front of him. Not that he could see. The beds must have been laid out well away from the fire. He took another few steps forward, leaving the horse ground-reined behind him.

"Hello," he called again, a little louder this time.

A cold chill of warning raced up his spine. He was on vacation, he was not working, he was hunting no one and felt at peace with the world. Yet . . .

Raider dropped to his knees, and the Winchester snapped into a port-arms position across his chest, both hands on the stubby rifle.

There was no sound. No motion.

The fire a few yards before him flared briefly, then was no more than red glowing coals with now and then a low tongue of live flame playing across them. There was almost no light from the fire any longer.

Raider felt suddenly cold. Slowly he eased down, presenting no silhouette, making of himself virtually no target at all.

This didn't feel right.

And long and sometimes bitter experience had taught him that it was better to make an ass of himself a hundred times by needlessly wallowing in the dirt than just once to make a target of himself standing upright.

He thought he heard . . .

A tiny rosebud of bright light appeared off to his left and quickly blossomed to full flower, sending a lance of fire in Raider's direction.

He saw the muzzle blast in the darkness and half a heartbeat later heard the dull, booming report.

It was a rifle that had fired, not a revolver, and a large-caliber rifle at that. Something heavier than a .44-40 saddle gun. More likely a .50-70 or even one of the old Sharps .50-110s.

There was only the one shot. So the marksman probably felt sure of himself. Yet Raider heard no slug sizzle past his ear, heard no whining, quavering song of ricochet.

He pressed himself closer to the sunbaked earth and waited for the unseen rifleman to make the next move. Raider was too close to the little light that remained from the dying fire. He didn't dare stand up or even try to shift to a new position without giving himself away.

But this was a game he had had to play before. He knew better than to be in a hurry now. He lay where he was and waited, Winchester held at the ready.

Behind him the horse moved about, shuffled its feet nervously back and forth.

Raider turned to try and see if he could tell where the horse was looking. The animal's senses were more finely tuned than his. It could well be watching the stealthy approach of the gunman, or even that of a second shooter. It was always possible that the first had fired a blind shot to draw Raider's attention just so his pard could get in a killing slug.

Bullshit with that, Raider thought grimly. They weren't playing with a pilgrim here, and these sons of bitches had best be good at it if they figured to win.

He looked toward the horse again and was rewarded with the good fortune of a flicker of live flame from the dying fire, brief but enough to let him see the front end of the horse, which continued to shuffle back and forth nervously.

Oh, shit, Raider thought.

For the first time he felt a clenching of fear deep in his gut.

The fear he felt now had nothing to do with his own safety.

The horse was not peering out across the grass toward some gunman.

It stood head down and spraddle-legged. Weaving unsteadily. Fighting a losing battle to maintain its balance.

The animal's muzzle was held low to the earth. Strings

of pale snot hung down from its nostrils. Snot and—thick, dark, nearly black in the dim light—blood.

That sonuvabitch had shot at the horse, not at Raider.

All caution abandoned Raider now. He lurched to his feet, completely unmindful of the target he was making of himself. His heart was pounding furiously, but somehow he forced himself to avoid the madness of a full-out dash, made unwilling muscles respond by bringing him into a long, ground-covering lope that he could maintain all the way back to the house.

Because there was only one possible reason he could think of for anyone to pull him away like this and then shoot his horse.

And that reason was Lucinda McCollum.

He ran through the night, back the way he had just come. He ran with a cold, hopeless fury lying icy and knotted in his gut.

CHAPTER THIRTEEN

Weatherbee was more puzzled than ever. Emilie von Hausen was gone, headed home for Baltimore—typically, for Emilie, by way of San Francisco—on the afternoon northbound. But Doc's twice-thwarted shadow was once again very much in evidence.

Even though Doc had made a point of walking down to the depot to see Emilie safely off, after she had been told about the possibility that her conduct was being observed, the little man had stuck with Weatherbee throughout the remainder of the afternoon and into the evening.

Now Doc was in the gentleman's smoking room at the Antlers. The room, with its clublike atmosphere of fine wines, pale leaf tobacco, and superb brandies, was available only to guests of the hotel and personages of some importance. Doc found it interesting to note that the shabby little watcher was unable to join the gentlemen in the private room and had to maintain his watch from the public area beyond. Still, the fellow was persistent if nothing else.

His continued presence, though, now that Emilie was no longer on the scene, made Doc more curious than ever. He really had expected the man to disappear once Emilie was gone. He had not. Weatherbee was becoming annoyed.

Doc cupped his snifter in his palms, raised it to his face so he could inhale the excellent aroma drifting off the gently warmed fluid, and took a sip, finishing the beverage.

Immediately a waiter appeared at his side to remove the

empty glass and offer a rosewood box of hand-rolled cigars.

"No thank you."

"Very good, sir," the waiter said brightly, even though the man would have no reason in the world to care whether the gentleman chose to smoke or not. It was all rather silly, Doc reflected. But nice.

He thought briefly about having another drink, then rejected the idea. The fact of the watcher's presence, felt even when the fellow was unseen, was taking the edge off Weatherbee's pleasures.

If this kept up, Doc thought, the entire vacation was going to be ruined.

Damn the man.

Weatherbee came to his feet quickly.

Enough was enough, by Godfrey. He grabbed his hat and walking stick from the rack near the smoking-room door and walked with swift purpose from the room, out through the lobby and onto the street.

He did not turn to see if the watcher was following. He was sure the fellow would be.

And that was exactly what Weatherbee wanted now.

He wanted answers.

The game thus far had played out much more than was necessary, and nearly all of it to the watcher's wishes.

Now it was time for Weatherbee to make direct inquiries, and to hell with the guesswork.

Once again Doc turned uptown, walking quickly but this time making sure he did not go so fast that he might lose the man. He had no intention of outrunning him. Not this time.

Gas-fired streetlights illuminated the downtown blocks, but at this time of night all the buildings were silent and empty, the windows dark.

There would be people and activity down at the depot, of course, and quite probably also at the theater on Bijou. Doc avoided those and went instead into the shadowy paths of the small park on Tejon Street north of Bijou.

In the center of the park there was a gazebo almost large enough to be a summerhouse. On summer evenings there were public concerts given there, with the townsfolk gathering on the grassy lawn on all sides of the gazebo. This late in the season, though, the white pillars and latticework were empty of people, and the shadows under the roof were deep.

Doc took the pathway around the gazebo, then darted back as soon as he would be out of the watcher's view and mounted the three steps to the interior of the gazebo. He tiptoed silently across the stone floor of the structure to the side he had just come from and waited there.

Weatherbee had been walking swiftly, and the follower had to move along quickly as well. Doc spotted him on the far path within seconds after he had gained the shelter of the gazebo.

The fellow reached the edge of the shrubbery that had been planted along the path and looked to both sides but came on without hesitation. Weatherbee was out of his sight, and he would have to hurry to keep his quarry in view. He had been fooled once by speed and obviously did not intend for that to happen a second time.

Doc waited until the little man was only a few paces away and moving smartly along, then stepped out of the shadows and quickly down the steps.

Doc's cane snapped up, its brass ferrule poised at the hollow of the little man's throat like a sword. And indeed the cane could do considerable damage if it came to that.

"Wha . . . ?" The little man halted, his face blank with surprise. "Is it my money you want, sir? Is this a robbery?"

He thought quickly, Doc acknowledged. And he was cheeky enough to try to run his bluff even though he knew full well that Weatherbee was onto him. But then, what choice did the fellow have? The truth, Doc hoped. That was what he was after here.

"You know well enough what I want, sir, and it is not your money."

The little man smiled and spread his hands, as if to say that he was fairly caught and might as well go ahead and make a clean breast of it.

"A moment of your time," Doc said. "A word or two. Then, sir, we can go our separate ways, yes?"

The little man smiled again and nodded. He looked like he might have given Weatherbee a bit of a bow except for the cane that continued to hover in the neighborhood of his Adam's apple. Doc dropped the cane tip to the path and stood in front of the fellow.

"Professional pride, Mr. Weatherbee, compels me to say that I was specifically instructed to make myself obvious to you. You never would have spotted me otherwise."

Doc had no comment on that, although he did have some professional doubts on the subject. Still, the man's pride was being salved here, not his expertise displayed.

"We both know about me, sir. It is my knowledge of you and your, uh, mission that has me curious."

The little man spread his hands again. "Surely, Mr. Weatherbee, you would not divulge information about a client under similar... circumstances."

"You are a detective, then? Though not a Pinkerton."

"I confess that I do not have the honor to be associated with the Pinkerton Agency, Mr. Weatherbee. But I am a private operative. And quite a good one, if I do say so."

Doc grunted. The fellow certainly hadn't done anything to prove that. Doc had to wonder if the man was telling him the truth so far, if indeed he had been told to make the tail a blatant one. And if so, for what purpose. "Go on. I'm listening."

"Ethics prevent that, Mr. Weatherbee. Suffice it to say that I mean you no harm. Believe me, I never would have accepted an assignment that would bring harm to the Pinkerton Agency or any of its operatives."

"I need some answers, sir," Doc insisted.

"My apologies, but—"

The sentence was never finished.

From the shrubs thirty yards or so distant, the loud, abusive sound of a gunshot roared in the night, and the little detective pitched forward, striking Doc around the knees and dropping him onto the path on top of the little man.

Doc rolled toward the stone foundation of the gazebo and scuttled quickly backward into the protection of the low plantings that lined the structure.

By then there was no need, though.

There was no second gunshot.

Weatherbee could hear only the swift pounding of fleeing footsteps and soon afterward the shrill noise of a police whistle from a block or more distant.

By the time Doc got to his feet again and went to the side of the detective, the little man was dead, shot through the spine from behind.

Doc stared bleakly toward the dark buildings that surrounded the park. The assassin could have escaped into any alley or doorway.

And the little man who was dead at Weatherbee's feet would never tell his story now.

Bitterly Doc realized that whoever had been following the follower, whoever had been hiding in those shrubs, had been too far away to hear the little man's refusal to say anything about his employer.

Probably the gunman thought the detective was telling the Pinkerton man what he wanted to know.

The assassin's method of exacting silence was certainly effective, Doc acknowledged, if a bit crude.

He stood and brushed off the knees of his trousers, from where he had been kneeling in the dirt beside the dead man. He could hear the approach of footsteps and more whistles as uniformed police officers surrounded the park and began to enter it with revolvers held at the ready.

Doc had to stifle a smile, though. The officers came ahead with every appearance of ferocious readiness. But they had announced themselves quite thoroughly with the whistles before they came anywhere near the area of possible danger.

Doc held his hands well out to his sides and waited for the police to find him.

CHAPTER FOURTEEN

Raider stumbled, nearly fell, righted himself, and ran on. A sharp pain stabbed through his lungs, and his legs felt like they had been sheathed in heavy mud. In spite of his resolution to pace himself, he had pushed too hard, driven by fear for Lucinda, and now he was laboring. The worst part of it was that he was in no condition to get off well-aimed shots with the rifle. Not the way he was heaving and panting. Better the revolver than to depend on the steadiness of both hands at the same time. He transferred the Winchester to his left hand as he finally came close to the house. The big Remington felt solid and reassuring in his hand, and he wanted a target to turn it on.

He could see nothing, though. No one. Everything in the ranch yard appeared quiet and ordinary. Even the roosted chickens were silent. Lamplight formed a yellow rectangle in the yard in front of the open door to the house.

There were no intruders here. No shouting, looting men. Nothing.

Raider slowed nearly to a stop, bent over for a moment in an effort to catch his breath, and then walked cautiously toward the doorway.

But why, if... He shook his head impatiently. There was no point in guessing when a few more steps would give him at least some of the answers he needed. Whoever had shot the horse, and for whatever reason, there certainly seemed to be no disturbance here.

Raider wondered if now the rifleman was lying somewhere within range, waiting for him to silhouette himself in the lighted doorway and make of himself a perfect target.

He looked toward the house. Nothing *looked* to be amiss. He could hear nothing from inside. Not even voices, he realized now. He would have expected to hear Lucinda chatting with the boy, should have heard Kenny's bright, eager, nonstop conversation as he continued to tell his mother all the boring details of a perfectly ordinary day.

Raider heard nothing. Nothing at all.

The fears began to return.

He paused and looked into the darkness that surrounded the little house, but by now his night vision had been disturbed by his looking toward the lamplight. He could see nothing. Which was exactly what any rifleman would want.

Normally the thing to do would be to back away. Give his eyes time to adjust to the starlight again. Make a wide circle around the house to make sure no one was lurking with a rifle out there the way someone had been at the empty campfire.

But, damn it, Lucinda was inside that house. He had to make sure she was all right.

Piss on it.

Without warning, Raider sprang to his right, running for the side of the house. There was only the one way inside. The few windows were too high and too small for him to get through. If he wanted in he would have to go through the door. He didn't have to make himself an easy target, however.

He edged forward, back scraping along the cut sod blocks of the outer wall, Remington held at the ready.

While he did so he kept telling himself that he had heard no shooting while he was running back from the campfire.

But if Lucinda . . .

He crouched as he came closer to the open doorway, knowing full well that he was already bathed in the spreading light from the lamp inside.

Before a rifleman might have time to line up his sights —or so Raider hoped, anyway—he leaped forward and through the doorway, crossing it in a blur of motion and winding up indoors with his revolver ready and with his back again to the sturdy wall.

He saw no one.

No one.

Not Lucinda. Not Kenny. No one.

The pot Lucinda had used this afternoon to make a stew was empty now and lying on its side in the basin of soapy water. Lucinda's washrag was draped over the side of the basin. Kenny's drying towel had been crumpled and laid on the counter nearby, along with the dried but not yet stacked-away dishes and cups and tableware they had used.

"Lucinda? Kid?"

He looked up toward the loft, too small for sleeping purposes and used only for minor storage. It was the only place inside the house that he couldn't see. As far as he could recall, nothing there had been disturbed.

Lucinda and the boy simply were not here.

Raider looked around more carefully, slower this time. There was no sign of struggle. Nothing seemed out of place. Certainly there was no blood in evidence here.

"Damn," he muttered aloud.

Throwing caution aside now, more alarmed than ever, he left the house, walking through the lighted doorway in full view of anyone who might be watching, and hurried across the yard to the low barn.

There, for the first time since he returned, he could hear slight movement and low whispers.

"Lucinda?"

"Raider." Even in that single word he could hear the quaver of her voice. She had been crying. Now that he had returned, she began to cry openly and loudly again.

Raider ran inside to her.

Lucinda was sprawled on her back, spread-eagled, on the hay pile she and Raider had used for happier purposes so many times in the recent past.

Her wrists and ankles were bound with pieces of thin, tough cord, tied to whatever nearby support posts or boards her attackers had been able to find.

Kenny, blinded by tears and terror, was kneeling beside his mother, trying in vain to release her from the bonds.

The boy seemed to be trying very hard to ignore the fact that his lovely mother was naked, her pale body bruised and battered.

"Jesus," Raider blurted.

He pulled Kenny away, turning him so he wouldn't have to see, and gently pushed the boy toward the house. "Go heat me some water, son. Just warm, not hot, then put it in a basin and bring it to me here. And some soap and a washcloth. Don't come inside when it's ready. Just tell me and set it on the ground by the door. Can you do that?"

The boy nodded mechanically. Tears continued to flow down his cheeks, and some gray-white mucus had collected beneath his nose, but he seemed mostly in control of himself.

"Go on now, son." Raider urged him away with a gentle push, then turned and dropped to his knees beside Lucinda. He crammed the Remington back into his holster and pulled his knife to cut her free.

Her hair was a tangled, hay-packed mess, and her complexion was splotchy and unhealthy-looking between the bruises that had been inflicted on her.

Raider cut her free and tried to gather her into his arms, wanting to comfort her and soothe her and somehow make the ugliness go away.

When he touched her shoulder, though, Lucinda jerked like she had just been jabbed with a white-hot branding iron. She pulled away from him, rolling onto her side with her back to him and drawing her legs up until she was curled into a tight, protective ball. Her shoulders shook and trembled with her crying.

He tried once again to comfort her, touching her lightly on the shoulder. This time she cried out in bitter protest and once again reacted as if he had stabbed her.

"I...I...all right, I...won't try an' touch you... again." He felt helpless, unable to help and unable to kneel there idly without helping.

"What...can you tell me about it?" he asked hopefully.

Lucinda acted like she had not heard. She continued to lie in her tight-wrapped ball, rocking slightly back and forth and keening softly to herself as she cried.

Raider did not know how long that went on. He tried to speak to her, but she did not react. He didn't try to touch her again.

He heard Kenny's slow approach outside the barn and the sound of water spilling over the rim of the basin the boy carried.

"It's okay," he said softly. "Set it down." He hesitated. "Go back inside the house, son. We'll be along directly."

"Yes, sir." At least the boy sounded like he was in control of himself again.

Raider left Lucinda's side long enough to bring in the basin and soap and cloth he had asked for, but now he didn't know what to do with them. If he couldn't touch her...

He settled for putting the things down near her. "There's water for you to wash with, honey. If you want. I'll... be right back."

He hurried to the house, no longer even thinking about the possibility that someone might still be lying in ambush, and pulled a heavy blanket off the bed. Kenny looked at him but did not speak. Raider gave the kid a bleak look of utter misery, shook his head once, and ran back to the barn.

Raider covered Lucinda with the rough blanket. When he tried to tuck it in around her feet she cried out in protest. "I'm sorry, I..." He shook his head. He did not know what else he could do. He was willing and able to face down any man on earth, but now he felt at a loss and did not know what to do. "I'll be back in a minute."

He went back to the house and found a dull-eyed Kenny stacking the dried dishes and putting them away on the shelves where they belonged.

"Can you tell me about it, son?"

The boy nodded. Without expression or inflection, his voice as dull as his eyes, he told the story.

"There was four of them. They came... we thought you was outside, but they just walked in. Didn't seem in any big hurry or nothing. Never said anything at first. They acted like I wasn't even here. They took Ma by the arms an' walked her out to the barn. I... I run after them. I tried to kick one of them, but he just laughed an' shoved me down on the ground. If I'd had me a gun..." He did not finish the sentence. He hadn't had a gun. Raider had talked about getting him one but hadn't gotten around to it yet.

The boy could not have known it, but Raider was bitterly cursing himself for not leaving one of his own weapons with them.

"They took...an' did things to Ma. Bad things, Raider. They shouldn't've done things like that. An' they still didn't say nothing, hardly. They didn't even act like they was enjoying it. It was like... it was like it was what they'd come to do an' they wanted to get it over with." The boy looked up at Raider and for the first time he showed emotion in his expression. Anger. Bitterness. But mostly a deep puzzlement. "Is that what it's s'posed to be like, Raider? I..." He blushed. "I've watched animals, you know. An' thought about such. But I never...I mean...I never thought it'd be so mean an' cruel. Not no fun at all. Just that meanness."

"No, son, it isn't like that at all." Raider ruffled the boy's hair and waited for him to continue.

"Two of them done that, Raider. Quick, like I said, and mean. The others, it was like they was keeping watch outside. I guess maybe for if you was to show up. But of course you didn't." The boy's voice broke a little there, and Raider could hear the unspoken accusation in the hesitation.

"When they was done"—he paused and took a deep breath—"when they was done, one of them pulled me around an' leaned down so he was talking into my face, like. So I wouldn't miss none of what he was telling me. Real slow an' mean he said, 'You tell your pal Raider that we're sorry we missed him this time an' since he wasn't here we're leaving this here as kind of a message for him. Can you remember that, boy?' And I said that I could. An'"—Kenny was starting to cry again; he had held himself under a rigid self-control until now, but the tears were running down his freckled cheeks again—"an' then he made me tell it back to him. So I'd get it right when you came." He stopped to run his wrist and forearm under his nose and to snuffle loudly.

"An' then one of them at the door said something, I didn't hear exactly what, an' they all of them hurried outside, and the last one, he pushed me down. Real hard. And I started to cry. I hadn't been crying all that much till then, I swear I hadn't, I guess 'cause I was so mad but couldn't do nothing, an' then the bunch of them ran off, and then pretty soon you got back. And...I guess that's all I know."

Raider had listened carefully, trying to memorize every word the boy said. He listened almost with disbelief. Raider had known some sorry sons of bitches before. But this...

A kind of a message for him. *They had left a kind of message for him.*

They had violated his woman. May have destroyed her for all Raider knew. And it was a kind of message.

Raider shuddered stiffly, and his back straightened as he held himself erect. There was a deep, smoldering madness that showed in his dark eyes, but his jaw was set and his face was without expression.

What Raider was feeling now was not hate. It was nothing that simple. Nothing that easy. What he was feeling now was deeper. Quiet. And deadly.

They had left him a message. All right. He had gotten their message.

Now it was his turn.

Calmly, as if he had all the time in the world, Raider stroked Kenny's head and said, "I have to go back out and see what I can do for your ma, son. Then I'll come back in, and I'll want you to tell me everything you can remember about those men. What they looked like, what they was wearing, what horses they rode, what guns they carried, everything you can bring to mind, son. You study on it while I'm over to the barn, If you can, draw me pictures. Whatever you can think of. Will you do that for me, son?"

"Yes, sir."

"Good boy." Raider turned and went back out to the barn. Lucinda was sitting up now with the blanket wrapped around her shoulders. The soap and washrag he had put at her side had been used; the cooling water remained in the basin.

He reached a hand down to help her to her feet and was saddened by the look of terror that glazed her eyes when she saw his hand approach her. She shrank away from his touch, and in the one brief instant when their eyes met Raider could see raw, ugly loathing. For him. For all men, probably.

"I'm sorry," he whispered. It was a futile thing to say. Empty and worthless. But it was all he had to offer, and it was nowhere near being enough.

CHAPTER FIFTEEN

Raider was damned glad it was past sundown by the time he finally rode into San Sabastian. With any kind of luck no one would see him arrive.

Not that he was trying to hide. Especially from the men he had come here to find. He just would have been frankly embarrassed to be seen riding the poor damn pony that had taken all this while to make the trip. So he was glad enough under the circumstances that it was after dark.

His boots were not dragging the ground. But they sure felt like they might, with Raider's long legs dangling down over the sides of the scruffly little animal.

The kid's pony was a tough little son of a bitch, though. Small and slow but tough as rawhide after all the hard pushing he had done.

He found a public livery, thank goodness on the south end of town, and was greeted by a grinning kid not much older than Kenny who didn't even try to hide his amusement at seeing the tall, dark-haired man riding on a squat, round-barreled pony.

"Want me to tend to your, uh, horse, mister?" the boy offered.

Raider glared a warning at him. He was not in any humor for jokes at the moment. "Yeah, you can tend to it. Cool it off good an' rub it down, then water an' feed it slow-like. The little bastard oughta be about wore out."

"Yessir," the boy said soberly. He took the reins and held the little animal while Raider stripped off the big, ill-fitting stock saddle from the pony's back.

"Treat it right, boy, and there'll be something extra in it for you."

"Yessir," the boy said again.

Raider lugged his saddle inside the livery barn and tossed it onto a rack provided for that purpose. The boy, behind him, noticed that this tall, serious man checked to make sure his revolver was riding loose in its holster before he pulled his Winchester from the scabbard still attached to the saddle. The lean, darkly handsome man stood for a moment in thought, the Winchester balanced easily in his hands, then turned and asked, "Where would a man find a drink around here?"

The question surprised the boy. He would have guessed that this man was looking for something more than just a drink. "Right up the street, mister. There's a bunch of places to choose from. 'Less you're a Mex'can. They all do their drinking at a cantina off over that way." The boy pointed, but Raider ignored him. He was not here looking for any of the local Mexicans. The men who had attacked the McCollum place were Anglos.

"Thanks," Raider muttered. He headed up the street with long strides that covered ground at a deceptively fast rate. He did not give any appearance of hurrying. Rather, he seemed intent.

And he was.

Five men, he had concluded on the long ride up from the McCollum ranch. There had to be at least five of them. Four had been there at the barn for their ugliness. At least one more brushed up near the campfire to shoot down Raider's horse. There could have been more. He was sure there were no less than five.

Long odds, but fuck 'em. Raider did not care if there were fifty. However many there were, they were going to die, each and every one of them.

He was sure about that.

Most of the businesses in San Sabastian—there weren't all that many of them—were closed for the night, their windows dark and empty. He had no trouble following the nearest glow of light to the first saloon. Raider stepped inside and immediately began to assess the customers at the bar.

If the men were here—and he was damn sure hoping they were—he was at a disadvantage. If they knew enough about him to talk of him by name after they'd abused Lucinda, they likely had had him spotted. They should have seen him and would know him. He, on the other hand, had only a few sketchy descriptions to go on. Neither Lucinda nor Kenny had been clear about the descriptions, and much of what they had said was contradictory. That was common enough, of course. It had been dark. Both woman and boy had been terrified and under stress. The only surprise would have been if they had been sure of the descriptions.

There were fourteen customers in the saloon. No, fifteen. A drunk was passed out in a back corner. No one seemed to pay any particular attention in the newcomer.

The customers lined the bar in loose groupings of twos and threes and one bunch of four men who were talking together.

Slowly the men in the place became aware of the silent menace shown by the man at the door. Slowly conversations stuttered to a halt until the place was quiet. Someone set a shot glass down on the unpolished surface of the bar. The sound of glass meeting wood seemed unnaturally loud. One man standing at the end of the bar with his shoulder leaned against the wall turned pale and looked like he wanted to make a move toward the revolver at his waist but lacked the will to do so. Wanted, Raider thought. Wanted for some crime someplace and nervous now from his own guilt. Raider truly did not give a shit who the man was or what his crime had been. Unless, of course, he was one of those Raider sought.

"Is there..." The bartender's voice cracked, and he licked his lips nervously. He tried again. "Is there something we can do for you, mister?"

The fugitive at the end of the bar had begun to sweat.

"Five men," Raider said coldly. "They'd have rode in sometime earlier today. Afternoon, likely."

The man at the end of the bar squeezed his eyes shut in obvious relief. His knees sagged weakly, and he had to lean forward and put his weight on the bar to support himself. Raider continued to ignore him, his eyes boring instead into those of the bartender and the few men near him.

The bartender shook his head. "Haven't seen anybody in two weeks that I haven't known his name an' his family, too. Those as has family, anyhow."

"They could be locals, for all I know," Raider amended. "Five or more, riding together. They headed this way."

The barman shook his head again. "Not that I seen, mister. I'll swear to that."

The men standing in front of the bar turned their faces away from Raider and stood stiffly and in silence. Whatever this was, they did not want to be mixed up with it. The fugitive at the far end of the bar began to look nervous again. Raider could see the sheen of sweat break out afresh on his forehead.

"You," Raider snapped.

The fugitive turned panicky eyes toward the tall, angry stranger.

"Yeah, you." Raider gestured toward him with the muzzle of the Winchester, and the man went pale again. "What've you seen today?"

"Nothing," the man said quickly. Too quickly. His voice came out in a high whine, and he looked like he wanted to cry.

"Bullshit," Raider said. The single word was spoken softly but carried a tone that was as hard and as brittle as slate.

"I..." He gulped. "I seen...you know...some strangers. Didn' count them. I seen them a while ago. Over at Blue Ellen's."

Someone at the bar snickered. "That'll be the day. When he can afford Blue Ellen's prices."

"Shut up," someone else hissed in a whisper that carried clearly through the tomb-quiet place. "He does odd jobs there sometimes."

"I c'n just imagine how odd," the first voice whispered back.

"Where is Blue Ellen's?" Raider asked coldly, ignoring the other crap.

"Block over, two blocks up," the bartender said. "You can't miss it. She keeps a blue light by the door."

Raider nodded and backed out of the place.

Whatever the one fellow was wanted for, the fool had taken up the wrong line when he went to breaking the law. He hadn't the temperment for it, and before much more time went by he was sure to find himself in jail or else dead. For the moment, though, he had served the purpose Raider wanted. Raider was more than willing to leave the poor bastard alone to sweat out whatever days he had left.

Raider found the whorehouse easily. There weren't many horses tied outside it, but that meant nothing. He tried the door, found it locked, and knocked sharply.

The woman who came to answer it was gray-haired and ugly. She wore a blue dress, and even her hair seemed to have been washed with laundry bluing or some such because it had a faintly blue appearance to it that made her even uglier than she otherwise would have been.

"Yes?" She stood blocking the doorway, looking him up and down, taking in the dusty black boots, denims, time-worn leather jacket, and dusty black Stetson. She looked deep into Raider's dark eyes, nodded once, and stepped back to admit him to the place.

Before Raider had a chance to speak, Blue Ellen amazed him with a sharp bark of laughter. "You're early," she said. "I wasn't expecting you till late."

"Wha . . . ?"

The old harridan turned and screeched toward the back of the house, "Frannie? Frannie! That special gennelmun is here for you. Run get your dress, Frannie." She turned back to Raider. "She won't be a minute, honey. Like I said, we wasn't expecting you for a while yet."

Smiling, she took him by the elbow and tried to lead him inside.

Raider stood rooted at the door in confusion, but the bawd appeared not to notice. She chattered on. "Mr. Raider, is it? Come in, honey. Frannie won't be but a minute now. Could you tell me something, though, dearie? I mean, I know it maybe ain't any of my business, but I just got to ask. Is this here a present for you or some kind of a joke? Not that you got to tell me anything. But you know that, I expect." She continued to pull at his sleeve. "Just you come in now, honey. An' don't be reaching for your wallet. Unless you want to leave a little something extra, that is. Frannie's all paid for, you know. Or didn't you know?" She began to look worried. "Oh my. I might've gone and spoiled the surprise. I hope I haven't done that."

The old woman looked genuinely worried that she might have ruined a surprise for her guest.

She hadn't.

Raider felt the blood drain from his head when he saw the whore who appeared in the hallway now.

Frannie had bright red hair, an artificial shade somewhere between the bright hue of Kenny's and the rich auburn of Lucinda's hair.

She was red-haired, though, and from a distance her figure was not unlike Lucinda's.

There was no real similarity between the two woman, but the intention was clear enough.

Because the most stunning, the most damning thing of all was the dress Frannie was wearing.

It was the dress Lucinda had been wearing while she and Kenny were washing the dishes last night.

Not just a dress *like* that one but the *same* dress. Raider was sure of it. He could see where some of the buttons at the front had been replaced with others that did not match the originals. And it looked like someone had done a haphazard sewing job on a rip under the right arm.

But Raider would have sworn it was the same dress.

He tried frantically to remember the scene he had come on in the barn. Lucinda. Kenny. The ropes and stakes. He could not remember seeing her dress thrown aside there, and at the time it had not seemed to matter.

Now he was positive that those fucking animals had carried the dress along with them after they left the place.

Brought it here.

Paid this slutty whore with the red hair to wear it.

Jesus!

Shock and anguish and fury swirled through Raider's thoughts, numbing him. If the five men had stepped out of the whorehouse parlor just then they could have gunned him down, and he would have been unable to raise a hand in his own defense.

What were these bastards up to?

"Is something wrong, honey?" Blue Ellen was leaning close to him, a look of real concern on her wrinkled face. "Are you all right? Frannie, fetch me the smelling salts."

"No," Raider barked rudely. He pulled his arm away from the old madam's touch and held himself stiffly upright. "These friends of mine," he said softly. "Where are they now?"

CHAPTER SIXTEEN

Weatherbee laid his half-smoked Old Virginia aside, reached under the newspaper that was lying open in his lap, and consulted his watch. Just as he had thought. The police were late. They had arranged to meet him here at nine to take his statement about what he knew of the dead man, but they were late. It would have been annoying if Doc had anything important planned for the day. As it was, it was at worst a minor nuisance. He returned the watch to his vest pocket and was reaching for the cheroot when he was interrupted by the arrival of a page carrying a small silver tray with a folded Western Union message form on it.

"Mr. Weatherbee?"

"Yes?"

"Delivery, sir. Just arrived."

Doc thanked the boy, tipped him a half-dime coin, and accepted the message form. He grunted with surprise when he hefted the paper and made a mental correction. Forms, not form. There were several sheets of the yellow paper there. This message was a lengthy one indeed, which was most unlike the tightfisted head of the Pinkerton National Detective Agency.

He waited until the boy left, then took a look at the top page of the message.

This was becoming more and more curious, Doc thought. The message had been encoded so that no one outside the agency could read it. Moreover, he had quite deliberately refrained from letting either Allan Pinkerton or his nit-picking manager Wagner know just where it was that Operative Weatherbee intended spending his free time. Doc had not wanted to be bothered with unexpected intrusions from Chicago. And that was precisely what this looked like.

Frowning and inwardly fuming a bit, Doc laid the newspaper aside and carried the message form up to his room. The police were already late. If they still wanted to find him, they could look for him there.

He closed and locked the door behind him, then retrieved his codebook from the false bottom of his Gladstone. It was an article of equipment he had not expected to use for at least another full week. Still, it would be better to know what had prompted so great an expense. Pinkerton messages were usually kept as brief as possible. And Doc was certain he would not be badly overstating the case if he were to claim that he had seen dime novels shorter than this telegram appeared to be.

He lighted a fresh cheroot and sat down at the writing desk with the message form on one side and the open codebook in the other.

This was going to take a while.

Weatherbee frowned, leaned forward, and reread the message:

unknown gang baiting me, had opportunity to kill but did not try. hard sons of bitches. explain later. must apprehend. they riding relays of horses already posted to north. i riding nag, their plan. heading now taos. they mention manitou. your way. up to something but unknown who or what. i think your woman in danger there. send her to safety. immediate and urgent. send to safety. wait there. from taos i should know route they to follow. will wire you at antlers. want you to bring good horses, intercept gang. too much damage already done. must, repeat must, apprehend.

It was signed RAIDER.

Doc frowned again. The message said much. But not half enough. Obviously Raider did not know who these people were or what they wanted, but just as obviously he had some reason to believe that Emilie von Hausen might be endangered by them. What would have made him think that?

And *who* had had the untaken opportunity to kill whom? Had Raider for some reason turned down a chance to apprehend these people and now regretted it? Or had the gang rejected a chance to kill him? The telegram was unclear on that point.

"Hard sons of bitches." The language was typical Raider. But most unusual in a telegraphed message, even in code. The agency's rules, in accord with Allan Pinkerton's straitlaced beliefs and personal habits, tended to make every operative careful in his or her selection of wording in coded messages. That was a habit that would be difficult to defy under even the most trying of circumstances. Yet here Raider had done so.

Odd.

"Too much damage already done."

That, perhaps more than any other portion of the message, puzzled Doc. What damage? And why had Raider not given even the barest hint of detail about it?

Doc scowled. After a moment his expression softened. It would be pointless to worry about it now.

Emilie was already safely out of the way, en route to the East Coast by way of the West Coast. So she was all right.

It seemed suspiciously likely that the detective who was murdered while speaking with Weatherbee in the park had something to do with this plan.

According to the telegram, Raider's gang was mounted on relays of fresh horses, which meant someone had carefully planned whatever was happening to the south.

It seemed entirely possible that there was an arm of the same plan in operation here also.

Damn! The gunman who had assassinated the little detective could easily have killed Doc from ambush as well, Doc realized. He had not chosen to do so. It could have been some similar circumstance that Raider meant when he said an opportunity to kill had been passed.

Who, then? And why?

Doc would have given much to be able to talk with the little detective. Damn it.

Someone knocked briskly on the hotel room door. "Police to interview Mr. Weatherbee," a voice said.

"Coming."

Doc stood, hesitated for only a moment, and then swept the Western Union message forms under the blotter on the desk.

He crossed the room quickly and hid his codebook back inside the Gladstone before he answered the door to admit the two officers who were waiting respectfully in the hall.

Until he had a better idea of what was happening here, he had no intention of letting strangers in on his speculations. Not even the police.

"Yes, gentlemen. Come in, please."

CHAPTER SEVENTEEN

Raider loped into the relay station—ranch, actually; those pricks were only using it for a relay station of sorts—and brought the big roan to a halt. The animal was still in fresh and unwinded condition, so he let it water before he tied it and dipped his hands into the trough the horse had just used. The water felt cool and refreshing. He removed his hat and poured some over his head, allowing the liquid to trickle down his neck and sop into his shirt. Cold as it was at night here, the days were still plenty hot.

A man came out of the shed near the corral and when he saw Raider began trotting toward him, quick anger on the rancher's face. "Who the hell are you to make yourself free with my water?"

Raider looked him over before he bothered to answer. The man was a farmer, not a rancher. The few cows Raider had seen on his way in were spotted dairy-type critters and nothing that a man of this country would get proud over. Raider had been willing to give the man the benefit of the doubt and consider him a rancher, with herds somewhere out of sight, until he saw the raggedy overalls and twine-patched low shoes.

"Figured you'd be expecting me," Raider said finally. He pointed toward the corral where five worn but still handsome animals were resting.

Raider grunted with disgust when he saw that the horses, tip-top horseflesh as all of them had been, had not been brushed or curried since the gang switched their saddles to whatever animals they had had waiting here.

"Oh, it's you," the farmer said.

"Yeah, damn it, it's me. Any messages?" More often than not the smart-aleck bastards ahead of him left taunting messages. These men were really pissing him off. But right now there was nothing he could do about it.

"Nope," the farmer said. "But they left you somethin'. Said they thought you might be able to use it."

"What's that?"

The farmer pointed. In a near corner of the corral, almost hidden by a slant of shade, was a lop-earred burro.

The implication was clear enough: the bastards figured by now Raider would be on a horse so broken down by the pursuit that he would want to ride the burro.

Raider smiled to himself, his lips thin, his eyes deadly. Sons of bitches wouldn't know that he had run into that cowboy back down the road a piece. The cowboy had been willing to make a swap. His good roan for Raider's used-up nag. And fifty dollars in hard money.

It had been a hellish price but more than worth it if it allowed Raider to get a jump on the gang. Already over the past several days they had established a pattern. Run like hell between relays until they got impossibly far ahead of him, then lay over at a saloon or a whorehouse or both and give the near-frantic Raider time to *almost* catch up to them. Then off again on their damned fast horses to the next relay, with Raider flogging along behind as best he could. And always before they had been able to arrange things through one devious method or another so that he couldn't find, buy, or steal a decent horse to put under his saddle.

Well, this time he had foxed the bastards. This time he had the roan.

He was feeling proud of himself until he noticed something that had escaped him about the uncurried last relay that the pricks had left behind here.

This time the five horses, although still salt-caked on the quarters and matted where the saddle pads had been, this time the last mounts had had time to thoroughly cool off and dry before Raider got to the relay point.

So the gang was still far ahead of him.

Shit!

They couldn't know about the roan, though. They couldn't. That had to be worth something.

"Did my friends say where they were headed?" Raider asked. He had long since given up trying to explain the true situation to any of these relay tenders. All of them had been innocent dupes, hired, usually with the promise of being able to keep the tired horses left behind, with no idea of the seriousness of the venture they were abetting.

"Taos, they tol' me," the farmer said. "Ain't that where you was to meet them?"

Raider nodded. He was tired. Too many hours in the saddle. Too little time to stop for food. Sleep too lousy almost to be worth bothering with when he could stop. Mostly, he guessed, just too damn much frustration for day after day.

"How far to Santa Fe?" he asked, sure of the answer already but wanting to confirm it.

"Five mile. A bit more."

Raider nodded his thanks and mounted. There was no point in getting mad at this man. The fellow was an unknowing tool and not a part of the plan. Experience had already taught Raider that none of these people could add much to what he already knew about the gang.

Nick. Willie. Bray, which was probably a nickname, since he had a laugh like a mule's bray. Alonzo. And the quiet one whose name no one had heard.

Raider knew each of them so well by now that he could see them in his mind even though he had never yet seen them in the flesh.

That time would come, though. He was certain of that. He never let himself doubt it for a moment.

Each one of those bastards was dead and didn't have the sense to realize it.

"Thank you," Raider said again. He turned the good roan up the road toward Santa Fe and let the horse take a ground-eating jog.

He could have pushed the horse faster, but he had a decision to make and little time to make it.

He had to decide damned soon whether to push on

through Santa Fe and up the old road to Taos Pueblo. Or here, on the south end of Santa Fe, to cut east for Glorietta Pass and Las Vegas and the old Santa Fe Trail.

Here the main roads split, and a wrong decision could throw him hopelessly off the track.

If that happened he would still get the sons of bitches. That much was never in question. But if he lost them so completely, it could be months or even years before he could find them all, and then it would have to be a matter of running them down one at a time the hard and slow way.

He waited all of them. In a bunch. And right damned now.

Raider's eyes narrowed and his neck corded from the tension of just thinking about it.

He wanted them.

Bastards.

Up ahead he could see a fork and assumed that the right-hand road would lead over to Lamy, which was as close as the damned railroad came to Santa Fe—and wasn't that the shits; the Santa Fe Railroad never actually went to Santa Fe—and on to Las Vegas and Raton and Trinidad and Manitou. Or he could take the left fork on up through the city to Taos and Fort Garland and beyond.

Ever since San Sabastian the gang had made no bones about which way they were headed. They *wanted* him to know. Wanted him to follow them to Taos. They'd made that plain enough time and again to everybody they talked to.

That right there was enough to make a man suspicious. Laying that false trail made him think maybe this was where they were going to just thumb their stinking noses at him and break off from the route they'd made so plain to him.

But, damn it, if they were going to do that, why had they gone to all the trouble of deliberately pissing him off the way they were?

Why the quietly insulting messages calculated to enrage him all the further?

They went to a great deal of trouble and even some expense just to make damn sure he was so mad there was nothing that could make him leave their trail.

Surely they wouldn't have done that if they intended to try and slip away from him now.

He shook his head. None of this was making any fucking sense, but he had to figure they were genuinely headed for Taos.

The only thing was, once he found out about that for sure, maybe there was a thing or three him and old Weatherbee could do to throw some snags into their plans.

The hell with it, Raider decided angrily. The gang was still calling the shots for the time being. Raider had to go along with what he best figured.

He headed the horse left. Toward Santa Fe.

CHAPTER EIGHTEEN

As always, Santa Fe made Raider feel just a bit disoriented. New Mexico was a territory of the United States, and Raider knew that. But Santa Fe had a look and a feel about it that always made him think he must have taken a wrong turn somewhere and ended up in Old Mexico instead.

He threaded his way through the narrow, twisting streets, past adobe houses and adobe walls and adobe beehive ovens until he came to the plaza with the governor's palace—and where else in the country would a territorial governor have a damn palace for his office, and a low, adobe one at that?—off to his left, and La Fonda straight ahead on the far side of the plaza from him. At least now he could see a few Anglos on the streets. Not many, but there were some.

A bunch of Indians were clustered around in front of the governor's palace pretending not to pay attention to the traffic around them, and some freight wagons were rolling through with their Anglo drivers cussing at the Mexican kids who insisted on playing right under the wheels of the big rigs. It was almost enough to make Raider think he had taken a wrong turn in time, too, and that the old Santa Fe Trail was still operating. Except that these wagons likely hadn't driven any farther than the railhead down at Lamy. There wasn't much left of the trail these days but the ruts, although folks moving west who didn't have the price of a rail ticket still used it now and again.

Different. There was even a different smell to the place.

Cedar smoke and chilis. Nice. But different.

Raider pulled up in front of the old hotel where, hell, probably generations of Santa Fe travelers had stopped before him, and went inside. He was tired. Not just physically tired but soul-weary from thinking about Lucinda and those sons of bitches that were still ahead of him. His feet were dragging when he went inside La Fonda and leaned on the registration desk.

The clerk was a slightly built Mexican with gray in his hair and in a close-cropped trim mustache. He smiled broadly when he saw Raider.

"Señor Raider," the man said with obvious pleasure. "So nice to see you again."

Raider blinked and tried to remember. At first look he would have sworn he had never seen this man before in his life, although he had stayed here a couple of times before. It took him a moment to dredge the information out of some forgotten recess of memory. "Thank you, Señor Beneviento." Tired as he was, he felt kind of proud at being able to remember.

"You are alone this trip?"

"Yeah. Alone." Doc had stayed here with him before, he recalled now. The clerk certainly seemed to have no trouble remembering everything, even if Raider did.

"One room, then, for the Señor Raider." Señor Beneviento smiled and placed a room key on the counter between them. "You would like, perhaps, a bath and a barber?"

"That sounds awful good."

"I shall arrange it." Señor Beneviento pushed the key forward, then raised a warning finger. "One small thing, Señor Raider, if you please."

"Yes?"

"This time no large and angry gentlemen to be thrown out through the windows, eh? This time please to use the door. And open it first, if that would not be too much trouble."

In spite of his weariness, Raider had to smile. Yeah, Beneviento had a good memory, all right. Raider had forgotten all about that little tussle. "It's a promise," Raider assured him.

"Gracias, señor." Beneviento clapped his hands sharply and a boy of twelve or maybe thirteen jumped to take Raider's room key and saddlebags. The kid was dark-haired, dark-eyed, and stoutly built, but he reminded Raider of Kenny all the same.

"Thank you, Señor Beneviento."

"I shall have a tub and water brought to your room at once and call for the barber to join you there, yes?"

Raider nodded and trudged along behind the boy, who led him up to the small, dark room that had been given him. The kid deposited Raider's saddlebags on the foot of the lumpy bed and accepted the tip Raider gave him. He left, leaving the door slightly ajar so the tub and buckets of hot water could be brought in.

Yawning, Raider ambled over to the window and looked outside. The single window in this room was set high in the wall and was narrow—too narrow to permit a man to be flung through it. Raider smiled when he realized too that there was a broad, sloping roof just beneath the tiny window. Anyone thrown out of there could not suffer serious injury from the fall. Señor Beneviento was taking no chances on the welfare of his guests.

The barber and the tub arrived at virtually the same time. Raider stripped off and settled into the tubful of steaming water and let the barber give him a trim and a shave while he soaked. The comforting heat of the water relaxed him, easing aches and tensions that he hadn't even been aware of.

"There's some change on the nightstand," Raider said when the barber was finished and was packing away his soap and scissors and razors. "Take whatever's right."

"Gracias, señor."

"An' something extra for your trouble."

"Many thanks, señor." The barber paid himself and left, pulling the door shut behind him.

Raider sank lower in the tub, submerging most of his chest and leaving his knees sticking out of the cooling water. He closed his eyes. This was just too damn comfortable to leave. He was about half asleep and he knew it, and he knew that if he did drop off to sleep here he would only wake up in a tub of cold water and be miserable. But right now he simply didn't give a shit. He closed his eyes and let the warmth of the water seep into his muscles.

CHAPTER NINETEEN

Weatherbee flicked the edge of the Western Union message form, ran the ball of his thumb along it, then flicked it with a fingernail again. The message contained information, but it told him nothing.

The police had identified the dead man as Josiah Belknap, address and occupation unknown. Personal effects found in his room—at an inexpensive boardinghouse near the railroad depot and therefore near as well to the Antlers—gave no further information about the man.

Weatherbee had his own sources of information, however. He had sent a telegram to Wagner in Chicago. The response had been quickly forthcoming.

Belknap was indeed a private detective. He worked for himself, affiliated with no established agency, although he had twice applied to Pinkerton's for employment. His tiny, independent agency was headquartered—if it could be called that—in Cincinnati, Ohio.

Cincinnati. Doc could think of nothing, absolutely nothing and absolutely no one from that area who might possibly have an interest in Weatherbee's movements.

Or in Raider's.

There was still so much unexplained about that mysterious telegram from Raider, although common sense told him that there almost certainly had to be some connection between Raider's poorly explained warnings and Josiah Belknap's surveillance and death.

Damn it all, Doc thought. Damn it all.

A waiter, possibly reacting to Weatherbee's frown,

came quickly to the table Doc occupied and bowed slightly. "Sir?"

"What? Oh." Still frowning, Doc mechanically ordered tea, with lemon not cream, and continued to reflect on the problems of the moment.

He still had heard nothing more from Raider. Nothing since that encoded and confusing message of warning. Doc could not move again until he heard from Raider. He did not want to take a chance on missing the call for help when it finally arrived, so for the time being he was immobilized here quite effectively.

That was not a problem as far as the local authorities were concerned. They seemed to accept the idea—the simple truth, really—that the Pinkerton man had no knowledge of why J. Belknap had been murdered. In fact, they did not seem all that greatly troubled by the man's death. J. Belknap had been neither wealthy nor influential, and the local police seemed quite satisfied to chalk the murder up as an unsolvable but not particularly devastating happenstance.

Weatherbee was less inclined toward that attitude, but until or unless he heard again from Raider there was little he could do about it.

Now, though, the Pinkerton Agency was becoming curious. Doc had not offered any information in the request he had sent Wagner for information about the man, but the canny manager could not help but wonder why a vacationing operative, off duty and relaxing a good thousand miles from Cincinnati, would be wanting information about a small-time competitor like Belknap.

At the end of the reply from Chicago, Wagner had as good as asked Weatherbee for an explanation.

Doc only wished he had some sensible explanation that he could offer.

He sighed—he seemed to be doing that quite a lot lately—and accepted the cup of tea the waiter brought him.

Across the room from where Doc sat, an attractive young woman was also served tea and a small plate of scones still warm from the oven. Weatherbee was not paying attention to her and so did not notice the fact that she seemed to be watching him. If he had seen her eyes shifting so frequently toward him he would only have suspected that she was unaccompanied and possibly interested in a dalliance. The young woman certainly did not look like a detective.

CHAPTER TWENTY

At the sound of the doorknob turning, Raider's eyes snapped open.

They opened barely in time for him to see the door swing abruptly to the side, the knob crashing into the wall with a loud report.

Raider was still in the tub. The room was dark now, dusk having come and gone while he was dozing.

He was dozing no more. Spurred into immediate action by the loud intrusion into the room, Raider wrenched himself into a more upright position inside the cramped confinement of the portable slipper tub and flung himself sideways toward where he had piled his clothing—and the holstered Remington.

The zinc tub fell over sideways with a crash, and the cold water it contained spilled like a flood across the floor of the room.

Raider sprawled onto the wet floorboards, naked and slippery with soapy remnants of his bathwater. Even as he grabbed at the walnut grips of the Remington he could feel a small pinpoint of heat high between his shoulderblades, and he tensed, fully expecting to be shot there. He had time to wonder briefly if he would first hear the sound of the gunshot or if the first sensation would be that of lead slashing into flesh.

His hand closed on the revolver, and he whipped it around, thumb automatically responding to cock the weapon, the holster and gunbelt flying across the room.

He rolled onto his back and aimed the Remington

blindly toward the doorway, cocked and lethal. He lay on his back now, sliding a bit on the slippery flooring, legs sprawled apart, naked except for his own hair.

From the doorway he heard laughter. Then a gasp as the intruder realized the danger from the gun Raider was pointing.

"Raider! Darling!" she protested.

Raider blinked and struggled to sit upright, the revolver forgotten in his hand now.

It took him a moment to remember her. "Anna?"

"Yes, you lovely imbecile." Laughing once more, the woman shook her head in exasperation, then came inside and lighted the bedside lamp before she went back to the door and shut it against the light from the hallway. "I must say, darling, you haven't changed all that much." Her eyes were directed toward Raider's wet, flaccid middle. He was still lying there fully exposed, on his back with his legs spread wide apart. "And you do have a most exciting manner when you begin a . . . conversation."

"Anna!" Raider carefully let the hammer of the revolver down to safe-cock and tossed the blue steel weapon onto the foot of the bed. Then rather painfully—he must have bashed his side rather heavily when he came out of the overturned tub—he climbed to his feet.

"But it is good to see you again, dear."

"Damn, woman, don't you know any better'n this?" He found his gunbelt and returned the Remington to its holster, then searched the room for a towel and began to dry himself. He didn't feel any need to pretend modesty. Not with this woman.

She very likely would have been amazed, and appalled, to know that until this moment Raider had forgotten about her. After all, she was the, uh, lady over whom he had had that long-distant dispute that had led to another gentleman leaving La Fonda by way of an upper-floor window. But as before, the memories were coming back to him now.

"How'd you hear I was here?" he asked. He finished drying his ankles and feet, looked at the soapy mess on the floor, and with a shrug dropped the now damp towel into the middle of it all.

"Does that matter, darling?" She smiled at him coyly and began unbuttoning the front of her dress. Anna always had been direct, downright forceful even, about her pleasures. He was beginning to think that that hadn't changed any.

He stepped closer to her and took a moment to admire what she was showing him.

She had put on a few pounds since he had last seen her. But nothing serious. A bit more fullness in the hips. Maybe a touch thicker at the waist. But certainly nothing a gentleman would balk about. She was still a fine-looking woman.

And he was having no trouble seeing what he was looking at here.

Anna was down to garter belt and stockings at this point. Raider felt his response to the display, a quick, thickening surge of interest. Anna could see it quite as easily as he could feel it. She stopped what she was doing, and a smile spread over her pretty face.

"It has been an awfully long time, darling. But I knew you wouldn't be able to stay away from me forever."

"No," he agreed. "I couldn't." He couldn't for the life of him, though, recall if she had been all that good. In fact, except for that business about the fight he might not have remembered Anna at all.

Still with that catlike smile parting her lips, Anna came toward him, not seeming to mind that she was soaking the bottoms of her stockings as she walked through the puddle the bathwater had deposited on the floor.

She allowed Raider to take her into his arms, and her mouth was hot and receptive as she permitted him to kiss her. Her hands moved between their bodies to find and fondle him, then to tug insistently as she pulled him down onto the bed on top of her.

She was still wearing the garter belt and dark, opaque stockings. But, hell, he couldn't see any of that anyway from this angle. He certainly didn't mind.

Anna raised her legs, clamping them around his waist. She cried out with pleasure as he plunged inside her. She gasped, a loud, sharp outburst, and for a moment he thought he must have hurt her. When he paused, Anna shook her head violently back and forth and clutched at him with arms and legs alike, drawing him deeper into herself, demanding, eager, her hips pumping quickly to set the pace for both of them.

Raider was quite as eager as she was.

But he kept being mildly disturbed by a small question that was nagging at the back of his thoughts. He could remember the fight that time and that her name was Anna. But beyond that he couldn't remember a single thing about her. Her last name. How—why—he might have met her. Nothing.

After a few more minutes he really didn't care.

CHAPTER TWENTY-ONE

Raider walked into the saloon and took a chair at an empty table instead of pushing into the crowd that lined the long, fancy bar. He was still tired, but now it was the pleasant lassitude that comes from a good, draining romp in the sack instead of the deep weariness he had been feeling before. In many ways the unexpected encounter with Anna —her last name was Hurlinger, he had finally remembered, and she was the former mistress of a well-regarded army general—had been better for him than a night's sleep.

He felt refreshed. Much more important, his sense of near frantic urgency in the chase had fled along with his aches and sorenesses. His anger was no less, but it was better controlled now. He was willing now to plan for his revenge instead of merely reacting to the actions of the gang. And that difference might well prove a deadly one.

A painted bar girl in a short dress and ridiculously heavy makeup tried to get him to buy her a drink—and perhaps to buy her as well—but had to settle for bringing him a shot and a beer.

"Sure you won't change your mind, honey?" she asked when she brought the drinks.

"Not tonight, thanks." Or any other, Raider added silently to himself. Under all the makeup she looked like a homely bawd and a perfect candidate to be carrying the French pox or some such disease. He would have to be hard up to want any of that.

He drained off half the shot and followed the fiery

whiskey with a couple of swallows of the cool beer. The warmth of the combination spread nicely through his belly.

A man standing at the far end of the bar detached himself from the group he had been talking with and crossed the room toward Raider's table. He stopped a few short of the table, facing the seated Pinkerton man.

Raider leaned back in his chair and folded his hands over his stomach where both would be in full view. But close to the butt of the Remington. "Hello, Harry. I thought you were still making little ones out of big ones down at Yuma."

"Parole," Harry explained. "I was awful good behaved, you know. Rehabilitated an' all that shit." He grinned, but there was a wicked twist to the corner of his lips when he did it. And no mirth or humor whatsoever.

"Do tell. Well, I'm glad to hear that, Harry." Raider reached for the shot glass and took another small drink, then a short swallow of beer. He used his left hand to do the drinking.

"Some fellas was through here early today," Harry said. "They asked me to give you a message."

"Do tell," Raider repeated. He had more than a good idea of who would have left a message in Santa Fe for him.

Just a few hours earlier that thought would have infuriated him. Now he only felt a small spicule of ice laying hard and cold in his gut. "How'd they come to pick you for carrying their message, Harry?" The message itself would only be another taunt intended to fuel his anger, Raider was sure, but if there was some connection between them and Harry Coates maybe he could begin to make some sense of the whole thing.

"They didn't," Harry said. "I overheard them talkin' to another fella. That one didn't want to get involved." He grinned. The expression came out looking more like a sneer. "I wasn't so particular.'

"As I recall, Harry, you never were very particular. Or very bright either." Raider took another drink of his beer.

"The way them boys talked, I don't think they'll mind a whole hell of a lot if you turn up dead, Raider."

"What are you going to do, Harry? Shoot me? Not on

your best day, Harry. Don't you remember the last time? Shit, man, I took you without firing a shot. Waved a scattergun in your direction an' the next thing I knew you were down on your knees, Harry, blubberin' and bawlin' and begging me an' Doc to put the irons on you. And we done that too, you'll recall. Hauled you in for a fair trial in front of twelve men good an' true. What you'd best do, Harry, is leave well enough alone or this time I might have to hurt you."

Harry Coates was small-time. His idea of a big score was probably any drunk in an alley with more than two dollars in his pockets. He had gone to prison before when Raider and Doc found him among a gang of equally small-time bums who decided to take up stagecoach robberies and make high-living highwaymen of themselves. It hadn't worked that time, and apparently old Harry hadn't learned a hell of a lot from the experience.

"What you don't know, asshole, is that I learned a lot while I was down in Yuma. There's boys down there that could ream you a new one, Raider, an' they taught me a lot."

"I'll just bet they did, Harry. But not about guns. So what is this message you're supposed to deliver?"

"My friends said they might be just about ready to take you down, Raider. Might be Taos Pueblo. Might be La-Veta. You'll know when you see their smoke. But what they don't know is that you won't be alive that long, Raider." He chuckled. "Them fools paid me five dollars t' do something I'd be happy to do for free, y'see." His expression changed subtly, his jaw firming and his posture becoming stiff.

"Harry, I almost think you're going to try it."

"You son of a bitch."

Damned if he wasn't going to try it, Raider conceded silently. He waited.

Behind Harry Coates the crowd in the saloon had parted, clearing an alleyway of living flesh while the now silent men watched. In some mysterious manner the knowledge, perhaps transmitted by way of the tensions that flowed through Coates, had reached the bystanders. They knew. They were curious. They seemed eager to see the flow of blood from the loser.

"Helluva way to earn five dollars, Harry, buying it with your own life."

"You don't know, you bastard. I learned good. An' I've been practicing. Ever since I left Yuma I been practicing."

"You can still walk off from it," Raider said. "Think about that."

But Coates was done thinking. His hand, hardened and calloused by the handles of prison sledgehammers, flashed toward the Colt he carried low on his thigh.

Old Harry really had been taking lessons, Raider conceded. It was a picturebook draw, just the way it was supposed to be. Last three fingers hooking under the butt of the Colt. Thumb already pulling on the hammer. Hammer at full cock before the muzzle even dragged clear of the leather.

Perfect in every detail.

Except for one.

Raider was quicker.

Raider shot the son of a bitch in the chest. Then shot him again when Harry Coates did not go down with the first one.

Coates slumped to his knees, and the Colt dropped out of his suddenly nerveless fingers.

He looked at Raider with a growing disbelief in his eyes.

Then he was dead. His eyes became glassy and would see no more.

He pitched face forward onto the saloon floor. By then he did not mind the impact.

By then Raider was surveying the crowd behind Coates, making sure there was no one else in the crowd interested in picking up where Harry had left off.

There wasn't. Raider reloaded the Remington and dropped it back into its holster.

"Shee-it," someone in the crowd breathed.

Raider could barely hear him. His ears felt clogged from the jolting impact of concussion, and his nose was filled with the stink of powder smoke. It never ceased to amaze him now anything that smelled so good when out in the open air could stink so bad in close confinement. It would be days before the smell of the powder left him.

"Better, Harry, but you need more practice," Raider muttered to the dead man.

He tipped his chair forward onto all four legs, drained off the last of his shot and beer, and stood.

No one seemed inclined to argue with him if he wanted to leave.

He went back to La Fonda and went to bed.

CHAPTER TWENTY-TWO

At last. The forced inactivity—and, although he hated to admit it even to himself, his increasing concerns about that blankety-blank Raider—had been wearing on Weatherbee, weighing him down. At last he was free to move. To *do* something beyond mere sitting and waiting.

Doc folded the yellow message form he had just received and shoved it into his Gladstone. He would be traveling light, with only the case and such clothing as he might have taken on an assignment from the Pinkerton Agency. The big trunk with his formal wear and better things could stay here until his return. The cheerfully accommodating management of the Antlers would see to its safety in storage.

Weatherbee hefted the lightweight .38 Colt revolver that Raider despised so—but which was as effective as a cannon when properly applied—and dropped it not into the bag but into his coat pocket. It was becoming more and more clear that he might well have need of the weapon before this business was resolved. Whatever it was. That continued to remain in doubt, and Raider's wire had been no help at all in explaining things.

The wire simply told Doc to meet Raider in Pueblo, with fast horses and ready to ride.

It wouldn't have occurred to Doc to reject Raider's request.

Weatherbee finished his quick packing and closed the big trunk, leaving it in the room. Since he was taking only the one piece of luggage, he carried it downstairs himself and asked the room clerk to attend to the remaining things after he checked out.

"Of course, Mr. Weatherbee. Our pleasure. Shall we be seeing you again soon, sir?"

"I'm sure you will," Doc muttered, preoccupied with other thoughts at the moment.

He paid his bill and walked down to the depot. The next train south would be leaving in slightly less than an hour. That limitation on his time resolved the question of whether to look for horses here or in the steel town down on the banks of the Arkansas.

By late morning Doc had left the quietly gracious community of Colorado Springs behind him and was surrounded by the raw, rough bustle of a workingman's mill town instead.

By 1:00 P.M. he had managed to locate and hire a pair of exceptionally tall and and well-fed brutes that looked as though they had the leg, the heart, and the stamina to accomplish anything Doc and Raider might ask of them.

At 2:55 P.M. Raider stepped down off the smoker coach of a D. & R.G. northbound from Trinidad, Raton, Las Vegas, and points south.

The tall operative nodded when he spotted Weatherbee waiting for him, but there was no slapping of backs or silly grins. "You got the horses ready?" Raider asked as he approached Weatherbee.

"Yes."

"Then let's ride. I'll fill you in as we go."

"I certainly hope so." He noticed that Raider had a look of grim determination in his dark eyes, and his stride was unusually long if seemingly unrushed. Doc had to hurry to keep up with him.

Raider stomped past the horses Doc had left tied to the rail in front of the depot, and Doc had to call him back. "These two, imbecile."

Even for that, though, Raider had no comeback, although normally the taunt might have led to a quarrel.

Raider was well and truly upset, it was plain to see. Doc's curiosity, already at a high pitch, became all the greater. Raider quickly switched the rented saddle for his own and dropped the inferior livery article into the dirt. He whistled and motioned for a nearby teenage boy to join them, and Doc told the kid where to take the unwanted saddle. He let Raider pay the boy for the service.

"Now," Doc said when both were mounted and Raider had turned his horse toward the distant Wet Range mountains to the west. "What in hell has been going on down there?"

Raider told him while they moved.

CHAPTER TWENTY-THREE

"That's them, damn it. That's got to be them," Raider hissed. He laid the telescope aside and picked up his Winchester. He and Weatherbee were lying on a shelf of gravel behind a boulder that looked down over the old stage road, preempted by the rails now, that ran from Pueblo south toward Aguilar and Trinidad. South and west of where they lay waiting was LaVeta Pass, the route the gang had bragged they would take from Taos. But then Raider hadn't chased them as far as Taos. Once he learned the route they intended to take out of the massive San Luis Valley, he had wired ahead to Doc. And now the two off-duty Pinkertons were just where Raider wanted them to be, ahead of the five sons of bitches for a change.

"Put the damn gun down, Rade," Doc said in a normal tone of voice. "You can't know that these are the men we want. They could be any five cowboys riding off on their own business."

"Bullshit," Raider protested in a whisper, although the five riders were still a good two hundred yards distant. He and Weatherbee would have had to be shouting at each other with megaphones to be overheard by the five horsemen at this point. He took a careful rest against the top surface of the gray boulder and aimed at the rearmost rider. Start picking them off from the front and they would likely bolt back the other way and out of range. Start at the back and he might well spook them forward into an easier killing distance.

With a grunt of anger Doc slapped the barrel of the

Winchester aside. Raider would have beat the shit out of Doc for that except that they hadn't any time for it now.

"Damn you—"

"You don't know that it's them," Doc insisted.

"I tell you it is." Raider tried to take aim on the men again, but Weatherbee wrestled the rifle away from him.

"They're barely in range anyway," Weatherbee persisted. "Let me get a look at them." He picked up the telescope and held it to his eye with his elbows propped solidly on the rock. It took him a moment to twist and pull until he could get the instrument in proper focus. The men were much clearer to him then, as if they were no more than forty or fifty yards distant.

"I c'n tell you what they look like," Raider said.

"You've never gotten a look at them. You told me so yourself," Doc said logically.

"They was described to me, you asshole."

"All right, what do they look like?"

"One of them, prob'ly the one in the lead, is the one that I don't know his name. Big fella with a beard. Kinda grizzled-lookin'. Doesn't say much. There's another with a scraggly mustache and a scar beside his left eye. That one's Alonzo."

"I see one with a mustache," Doc admitted. "Can't make out if he has a scar or not."

"Then there's Nick. Short, blond fella, not too stout, wears a Webley Bulldog rigged for a cross-draw."

Doc grunted a confirmation. Nick would be the last one in the line of five.

Raider went on to accurately describe the others as well. Willie, skinny and looking something like a rodent with his pointy features. And big, sloppy Bray.

"All right," Doc grudgingly admitted. "It looks like these may be our boys. *May*, I said. We don't know for sure yet."

"Now what the shit d'you want me t' do, Weatherbee? Go out there an' ask them polite would they confess to being a bunch of rapists?"

"No," Doc said uncertainly.

Raider snatched the Winchester away from him, and

this time Doc did not struggle against him.

Much as it went against Weatherbee's grain to lie in ambush and shoot someone down, if anyone had ever deserved such treatment these five did. "We ought to be able to...." He shook his head. Right now he was not sure *what* they ought to be able to do. He took another look at Raider, saw the cold fury in his partner's eyes, and clamped his lips tight shut.

By now the five riders were little more than a hundred yards away.

"I can't let you do this, Rade. Not without even trying to take them legally."

Raider had his sights lined on the chest of the last man in line. On the man they called Nick.

"And we aren't truly certain that these are your men," Doc persisted. "What if you're wrong, Rade? It would be murder." He said it softly, without emphasis. Beads of sweat appeared on Raider's brow.

"They could be cowboys unlucky enough to look like your gang. Would you risk killing innocents? Would you risk leaving an innocent's widow alone? Like Lucinda?"

"Shut your fucking mouth, Weatherbee."

But Doc's gentle argument was beginning to tell on his companion. He could see that it was.

Raider hesitated. Then, with an oath under his breath, he fired.

The Winchester roared and bucked back against his shoulder, and down on the road a horse lurched to the side, staggered, and fell. Its rider, unharmed, jumped off the dying animal and rolled to safety behind a clump of yucca.

The other riders reacted quickly to the gunshot. They bent low over their horses' necks and scattered. Three of the men lined out in a hard run toward the west, toward the looming wall of mountains in that direction.

The fourth man whirled his horse and spurred it back toward his fallen but unharmed companion.

Raider raised himself into a kneeling position and touched off another shot, but his bullet went wide of the racing horseman. Or horse. Doc did not know at this point which Raider was aiming for. Regardless, he missed.

The fourth rider, the no-name man with the salt-and-pepper beard, pulled a revolver as he swept close to the downed horse Raider had shot.

Doc watched, incredulous, as instead of making any attempt to pick up the man on the ground, instead of trying to shoot back at Raider, who was in plain sight now, instead of any reasonable and logical action, the bearded man lowered the muzzle of his six-gun and fired point-blank into the face of the man who was rising from cover to meet the running horse that he quite obviously had expected to save him.

Nick fell over backward with his arms flung wide, and the no-name man thundered past the corpse and headed west in pursuit of the other riders.

"Jesus," Raider muttered. He shook his head, stared blankly toward the rifle in his hands as if he had quite forgotten about it for the moment, then raised the weapon into firing position and triggered a final shot toward the fleeing horseman. The range was impossibly long by then, though, and neither he nor Doc had any idea of where the shot went.

"Jesus," Raider repeated.

"Yeah," Doc agreed. He too felt shaken by this brutal and seemingly unnecessary destruction of a man who might have been saved. "Yeah," Weatherbee breathed again.

The disbelief, the sheer unexpectedness of it, kept them immobile for only a moment, though. "Let's go, Doc. Let's get those sons of bitches."

This time Weatherbee offered no protest that they might be chasing the wrong men. He and Raider both turned and ran down toward where they had tied their mounts.

And this time the gang's horses were no fresher than Raider's.

This time Raider expected things to go much differently than they had before.

CHAPTER TWENTY-FOUR

There was no thunder of flying hoofs. Practically no dust even. The chase likely would not even have looked like a chase had anyone been in a position to watch the two groups of riders without knowing that the two men in the rear were chasing the four in front with deadly intent.

Doc and Raider rode at a pace no greater than they felt was necessary, and the four men in front of them rode at a pace that was carefully calculated to gain the most speed from their horses without unduly tiring the animals. Both groups rode at a swift canter, no more than that, with Doc and Raider trying to very slowly come closer to the horsemen who were now riding some three quarters of a mile ahead of them.

"The sons o' bitches are good," Raider bitterly acknowledged. Doc was riding close at his side, upright and easy in the saddle. "But I think we can get them this time."

"Sooner or later," Doc said grimly. Weatherbee was feeling personally involved in the chase now too. It was one thing to be told about alleged past crimes committed by those men. It was another thing to watch their leader gun down one of his own companions in cold blood rather than risk the man's capture or the wearing down of a horse that would be required to carry double weight after a rescue attempt. And that was the only possible reason for the killing. Now Doc wanted them nearly as badly as Raider did.

The men continued to ride almost due west, toward the wall of mountain that lay on the south side of the Arkansas River.

"There's only the one pass that I know of up there," Raider said a few minutes later. "We might can catch 'em up in that. Our horses are fresher'n theirs, I think."

Doc nodded his agreement. The two Pinkerton operatives were careful to transmit no nervousness or sense of urgency to their hired horses. They wanted to take no energy out of the mounts that was not absolutely necessary.

The riders in front of them were distant but in plain sight. At an almost lazy pace the four animals reached a little-traveled wagon road and angled up it toward Wetmore and the pass toward Westcliff many miles ahead. They slowed somewhat as they climbed one of the innumerable rises in this rolling, nearly arid country. Doc and Raider held their pace constant, pulling a bit closer before the four riders disappeared on the far side of the low hill.

"Don't," Doc warned as he saw Raider shorten his grip on his reins and begin to lean forward over his horse's neck. "Not yet."

Raider frowned but accepted Weatherbee's caution. He kept the speed of his cantering mount loose and constant.

They reached the poorly defined and not deeply rutted roadway and angled into it, following virtually in the tracks of the four men. Here the gang had slowed as the grade began to steepen. Doc and Raider held their speed, however. Their horses were still breathing easily and were sweating only lightly.

"We'll be pickin' up on the sons o' bitches now," Raider said with satisfaction.

Weatherbee nodded but did not speak. He took more of his weight on the balls of his feet in the stirrups, making sure the horse was receiving that weight on the padded, comfortable bars of the saddle tree so there would be the least possible interference with the animal's movement. If they had had time Doc would have loosened his cinch and ridden on balance alone to give the horse the best opportunity to breathe freely, but that was not possible now.

Raider and Doc reached the crest of the low hill. Before them the road curved down slightly, then up again and around to the left, torward a few distant buildings that would be the community of Wetmore.

The town was a good two miles away.

And the road leading to it was empty. There was not even dust hanging in the air over its surface. Far ahead of them a heavy wagon was leaving Wetmore and heading toward them. But that was all they could see that was moving.

"What the...?" Almost involuntarily Raider's fingers closed on his reins and his horse dropped back into a jog and then to a complete halt. Doc stopped beside him.

Raider continued to stare in disbelief up the empty road.

"There." Weatherbee pointed off toward their right, to the north, toward the hidden course of the Arkansas.

Raider looked in the direction Doc was pointing. There, well over a mile away and dropping toward one of the rugged coulees that cut through the countryside close to the mountains, they could see the four remaining members of the gang.

The men were riding at a hard run now, dust billowing up behind their horses.

"Hot damn, they've turned rabbit," Raider shouted. "They're fixing to fort up someplace over there."

"I don't know," Doc disagreed. "They haven't played the fool before now, and they're using their horses at a fearful rate. They must have something in mind."

"So do I." Raider yanked his horse around and applied spurs to the animal's flanks. The animal bolted forward, leaving Weatherbee to discuss their prospects with a quickly settling puff of dust.

"Damn you," Doc shouted. But he had little choice except to follow Raider's excited lead. He kneed his horse into a lope and then gradually picked it up into a gallop as he tried to stay close to the excited Raider.

The gang had a good mile and a half on them now, but their horses had to be tiring rapidly. Doc kept telling himself that.

But he had a nagging sense that the men were not doing this from any sense of panic. The move, whatever it was, had been carefully planned.

Raider dashed across the hard, caliche-like ground, flying over pale brown grass stubble, slipping and scrambling across loose rock as they dropped down into the coulee and followed it. Doc rode eighty yards or so behind him, not willing to use up his horse just so he could reach Raider's side again.

They could no longer see the gang in front of them, but the path the men had taken was clear enough in the softer, looser dirt at the bottom of the coulee. They followed the dry wash for the better part of two miles, then easily saw where the running horses had climbed out of the cut at a place where the bank had been broken down at some time in the past. Doc didn't like the way his horse was sweating by the time they reached that point. He could feel the sides of the animal's barrel heave as the horse huffed for fresh air. Before long...

"Oh, shit," he heard Raider shout. Raider, ahead of him, was already out of the coulee. He pulled his horse to a stop atop the broken bank, and Doc slowed his and let the animal walk up the soft, crumbly bank to reach Raider.

"Son of a *bitch*," Raider moaned.

As soon as he left the coulee Doc could understand the cause for Raider's dismay.

In front of them, little more than a quarter mile distant, there were the ghost-town remains of what must once have been a small settlement of some kind. Now the old buildings had begun to tumble apart. A few were preserved and apparently still in use as a ranch headquarters.

"Hardscrabble," Weatherbee muttered as he reached Raider's side.

"What?"

"Never mind. It isn't important."

Nor was it. What was important was that now there was a corral built where the center of "downtown" Hardscrabble would once have been.

And in that corral, standing head-down and lathered with crusted sweat-foam, were the horses the four gang members had been riding.

The four animals stood bunched in a corner of the corral as far away as they could get from a fifth horse that lay near the gate in a pool of fresh blood. The dead horse showed no sweat on its gleaming copper flanks.

"Those cocksuckers had five fresh horses here," Raider said. "They killed that'un so's we couldn't use it."

"Jesus," Weatherbee breathed. Shaking his head, he nudged his mount into a slow, weary walk toward the corral.

"Where're you going?" Raider demanded. He obviously was anxious to resume the chase. And the trail the four men had taken ran toward the north.

"We have to rest these horses and water them, Rade, or they'll die under our saddles."

"But—"

"No," Doc barked sharply. "They've outsmarted us. Now we have to rest these horses or lose those men completely. And I will *not* lose them."

Raider obviously didn't like it. But he had no choice but to agree. Weatherbee was right. If they continued the chase now, with the four gang members mounted on fresh horses and Raider and Doc trying to continue to chase them on jaded, used-up animals, there was only one way the chase could end. And Raider didn't want to lose them either.

"How in hell did they know we'd jump them back there?" Raider grumbled as he joined Doc in the slow trek toward the water trough.

"They didn't have to know exactly where we'd wait for them," Doc reasoned after a moment's pause. "Or even that we would get ahead of them like that. They might have had fresh horses placed at a dozen different points along the entire Front Range, waiting for them in the event they were needed. The unused remounts we simply would never know about." He hesitated again, then said softly, "They're well prepared, Rade. Someone has given this a great deal of thought."

"Spent a shitpot full o' money on it too," Raider said. His voice and expression were sour enough to turn cider into vinegar.

"Yes," Doc agreed. "But why?" He shook his head. "Personally, Rade, I haven't a clue."

Raider dismounted and began to loosen the cinches of his saddle. "That's one o' the differences between you an' me, Doc. You always want to know the why of every damn thing. Me, I don't give a crap why. I just want those bastards." He gathered a handful of dead grass from beside the foundation of a fallen-in dugout and began to rub the sweat from his tired horse.

Weatherbee unsaddled too and tended to his horse.

CHAPTER TWENTY-FIVE

"Sure, I know the fellas you mean," the hostler said. He was busy—more or less—lazily rubbing oil into a patched set of light harness. "One of them, the man with the beard, he came around last month. Brought his horses, five of them, in on the train and hired me to board them for him. Dollar per day per head." The man's tone of voice changed, and there was something like a sense of awe that came into his eyes. "Paid me in advance. Cash. A hundert fifty dollars." He shook his head. "Then this morning when they left here they only took four horses with them. The other's out back there, the big dun with the tiger stripes on its forelegs."

Doc looked at Raider. He was sure they were thinking the same thing. *The gang had left here only this morning.*

It was two days earlier that the men had given them the slip at what was left of Hardscrabble. He and Raider had had to wait overnight for a train out of Florence once they finally got back on the gang's trail. Which, Doc was forced to admit, had been all to easy to do. It was as if the men were trying to leave information of their whereabouts, not at all as though they were trying to get away.

"How long ago'd they pull out?" Raider asked, his manner pretending that the question was of no importance.

The hostler shrugged. "Three hours. Something like that."

"Did they, uh, say where they were going?"

"Not exactly." The man dipped his rag into a pail of fluid that smelled like neat's-foot oil and rubbed at the leather srap he was holding. "Said something about heading north. I know they took the trail up that way."

Doc walked to the door of the big barn and looked up at the mountains to the north. The mountains this far up the Arkansas were not all that high, but they were frightfully rugged and nearly barren of vegetation. Farther to the north, he knew, the slopes were forested with fir and spruce, but here along the free-flowing waters of the great river the surroundings were bleak and sere. It was poor country to travel through. And ideal for an ambush if that was what the gang finally had in mind.

"Where does the road lead?" Doc asked.

The hostler shrugged. "Depends. Not much of anywhere nowadays, though there used to be a few hard-luck mining camps up in that country. Fella might be able to find his way on acrost to Buena Vista or up to South Park, depending on which way he wanted to go."

"But these, uh, gentlemen didn't say where they were going?"

"I already told you they didn't," the man said testily. The men he was being questioned about now were, after all, good and valued customers who had paid cash in advance to board their horses. He obviously didn't care a thing about the Pinkerton credentials Raider had shown earlier.

"What were their instructions about the horse they left behind?" Doc asked.

The hostler gave them a smug grin. "Said I could have him for my troubles. Signed him over to me with a bill o' sale and everything." The man's eyes widened as a thought came to him and in a less certain voice he asked, "You boys, I mean you bein' Pinks and all, you ain't saying that the horse was stole, are you?"

"Nothing like that," Doc assured him, "but I would like to see the bill of sale. You say it was the bearded man who wrote it out for you?"

"I didn't say, but that's the one." The man laid his harness aside and went inside the tiny office that doubled as a feed room. He returned a moment later with the paper and thrust it into Doc's hands.

The instrument was made out in a clear and legible hand, but the signature was an indecipherable scrawl at the bottom. It told them no more than Doc had expected, if considerably less than he had hoped.

"And they didn't say where they were going?"

"Nope." Now that the momentary fear had been assuaged, the hostler was becoming balky again.

Weatherbee motioned for Raider to join him, and the two walked out back to where they could see the abandoned dun. And to where they were no longer within the hostler's hearing.

"They want us to chase them into those mountains," Doc said.

"Sure as shit looks like that," Raider agreed. "But this time it's gonna backfire on the fuckers. This time we'll be on fresh horses again."

Doc shook his head. "They already know that, Rade. Lord knows, they haven't been stupid up until this point. You would be foolish to think they don't realize that now."

"So what's your point, Doc?"

"My point is that this whole thing is being played out according to their rules. We have to break that pattern. Now. If we blindly follow them into those hills, Rade, we may lose our last chance to do that."

"I don't know, damn it. We know they rode up that trail three hours ago. We got no idea where they're heading. We *got* to follow them. Got no damn choice about it. They could come out anywhere if we don't."

Doc shook his head again. "Damn it, Raider, that is precisely the kind of thinking I want to avoid here. They are dictating our actions. We cannot continue to do what they want us to do. We have to take the initiative. And we have to do it now. While we still can."

"I don't know," Raider said, the doubt clear in his voice. He turned and looked up into the low, barren mountains in the direction the hostler had indicated.

"They have something in mind," Doc said. "That's perfectly clear. Probably they have fresh horses posted for them somewhere up that trail, just as they have had to the south. If we follow them, we'll be afoot or not better than that whenever they want us to be. Because they'll continue to set the rules. No, Rade, what we have to do is jump ahead of them. I say we should take the train upriver. We can take the cars to Buena Vista and ride back this way. Pick the spot for ourselves, on our terms, and wait for them to come to us."

"Too risky," Raider protested. "They don't have to be heading for Buenie. They could turn off an' come out at Salida. Or on up to South Park. Or who the hell knows where else. We could lose them entire if we done that, Doc."

"It's a gamble," Doc admitted, "but if we just set off after them again we will have accomplished nothing. We will still be doing what they want us to do. They're too smart, Raider, and too ruthless to chance giving them complete control over the situation."

"No," Raider said stubbornly. "I won't gamble on losing these bastards. I just won't do that, Weatherbee."

"You must," Doc insisted.

"Don't try and give me any of your bullshit, Weatherbee. You ain't in charge here. Not of me nor anything else. And I say we can't take a chance on losing them."

"And I say we have to throw the dice."

Raider set his jaw in that bullheaded way that he had and sullenly shook his head.

"We *have* to," Doc repeated.

"No. Not this time, Doc. Not with these sons of bitches. Not after what they done to Lucinda. I won't chance it."

"You chance your life if you don't."

Raider snorted. "That's what I'm figuring to do, you asshole. That's just what I *want* to do. Put mine up against theirs and *win*. The bastards."

"Listen to me, damn it."

Logic met the resistance of simple stubbornness, and the discussion quickly degenerated into argument, and argument into fury.

In the end Weatherbee walked alone back down toward the railroad depot and the next train upriver to Buena Vista.

Raider took his hired—and now rested—horse alone onto the trail the four gang members had used little more than three hours earlier.

Raider was making a serious mistake. Doc was certain of that. It was a mistake Doc refused to participate in. Damn him.

Doc knew good and well that Raider's taunts, nasty insults some of them, and his threats to go on alone if Doc was too frightened to join him were all intended to force Doc's hand and make him come along where Raider insisted.

That would have been all right, except that that same path was the one the gang too insisted they take.

And that Doc refused to do.

So he returned to the railroad depot alone, bought himself a newspaper, and sat on a hard wooden bench to wait for the next northbound.

He didn't even watch while Raider rode alone up the narrow, stony trail into the rugged red mountains north of the Arkansas River.

CHAPTER TWENTY-SIX

That damned smartass Weatherbee had been right about one thing, anyway. This was turning out to be a repeat of the same old shit that had been going on ever since he took off from Lucinda's place. The gang was up ahead somewhere, not too awful far off, but running barely fast enough to wear Raider's horse down to dogmeat and just far enough that their own horses were used up right about the time they came to a fresh bunch posted ahead of them.

Raider reached the first such relay point late in the afternoon. What he found there purely sickened him.

Apparently the bastards hadn't felt they had used up their last mounts fully enough this time, so rather than take a chance on Raider being able to get some use out of the horses they were leaving behind, the sons of bitches had shot all four animals and left them lying there on the ground—those four and a fresh, unused fifth animal that would have been intended to carry the man that was lying dead back there east of Wetmore.

There was no sign of whoever had stayed here to tend to the relay of fresh horses, although someone must have taken care of them. A crude stockade had been built of aspen poles to hold the horses, and off to the side there was a lean-to where the camp tender must have stayed.

At least here the country was beginning to take on some green to it, beginning to look more like regular mountains instead of just being the sun-dried rock and baked red gravel that lined the river down to the south.

Raider did some cussing of the men, then added a few

words for that weak-sister Weatherbee and let his tiring horse drink from the tiny stream that ran nearby. He hated like hell to keep pushing the horse, but, damn it, he had no choice. If he let these men get away now...

He let the horse rest for a few minutes, mumbling and bitching the whole time because of the enforced delay, then got back in the saddle and headed on after the bastards.

They were *not* going to get away from him this time.

Raider rounded a bend in the switchback trail and began to grin. Down below him, surrounded by golden yellow aspen, there was a bit of a stream and along the south bank of it a patch of grass, some of it still green from the seepage of underground water from the creek.

But the best part of it, the thing that caused Raider to grin, was that there was a camp set up right at the edge of that green patch. A camp and a fire and a man hunkered down beside the fire fixing himself some coffee or whatever.

It wasn't any of the men Raider was chasing. He was close enough that he could see that. There was only the one cowboy there and not too far off a handful of calves that the man was likely driving someplace.

But the fellow had two horses with him. Both of them mighty good-looking horses.

And both of those good-looking horses nice and fresh and rested.

Hell yes, Raider told himself. And this time *he* would be the one with the fresh horseflesh between his knees.

This was a change those pricks wouldn't know about. He hustled the tired rental horse down the trail as fast as he dared take it.

"Howdy," the cowboy called as soon as Raider was well within hearing.

"Howdy yourself."

"Light an' set, mister. I got coffee and beans cooking. Glad to share with you."

"Thanks, but... I'm tryin' to catch up with some other fellas. Could be they passed this way a couple hours ago."

The cowboy shrugged. "Wouldn't know if they did. I

just come down off the Johnnyroost," he motioned vaguely in the direction of the low peaks to the south. "Haven't been here but long enough to get my fire going."

Better and better, Raider told himself. The gang would have no suspicion that Raider would be mounted on a fresh horse now. Not if the cowboy hadn't gotten to the little park yet when they passed through it. They would not have seen the man. Or his fine horses.

"Look, I'm really needing to catch up with these men. It's important. I'd like to make a swap with you for one of those animals of yours."

The cowboy walked closer and didn't try to hide the fact that he was appraising Raider's horse. "Good-lookin' animal," he said, "but about wore out."

"You won't be moving in such a big hurry with those calves in front of you," Raider reasoned.

"Naw, I won't," the cowboy admitted.

"And you see for yourself that this's a good horse. Just needs to take 'er slow for a day. As good a horse as either of those, I'd say."

"Ayuh," the cowboy admitted in a slow drawl.

"I'll make it worth your while. Give you..." Raider dug a fist into his pocket and came out with most of the little money he had left. He was not big on savings and never had been. "I'll pay you... forty dollars. Plus my wore-out horse."

The cowboy seemed to be considering it.

"It's important," Raider said.

The rented horse was not exactly his to swap, of course, but he could sort that out with whatever place Doc had rented the thing from later. This was the best chance he'd had yet to catch those bastards, and he didn't intend to lose it. Not because of the ownership of some hired horse and not because of the whims of some mountain cowboy. If it came to that, well, he would just *take* the fresh horse and worry about squaring that later too. He had to. He had no choice about it.

"Please?" Raider asked.

"Aw, what the hell. Why not. Forty dollars, you say?"

"I do." Raider handed the pair of double eagles over

before the man could change his mind.

"Take the tall red'un then," the cowboy said. "I been using him to carry my packs, but he's a good saddler too. Strong, he is, an' used to the mountains. He'll get you where you're going."

Raider nodded his thanks and quickly transferred his saddle from the worn-down rented horse to the leggy sorrel the cowboy had pointed out to him.

"Thanks," Raider said. And he had never been more sincere about anything.

This was his chance to put on a burst of unexpected speed and catch up to those sons of bitches. And he expected to do exactly that.

CHAPTER TWENTY-SEVEN

Weatherbee stepped off the train to the indolent, lazy atmosphere of Buena Vista. A few gawkers loafed on the platform, and a very few draymen consented to bring their wagons up to the freight cars so goods could be off-loaded and hauled up to the mining camps that lined the upper Arkansas Valley. There was undoubtedly a great deal of activity in the camps, but little of that showed in the small railroad town on the west bank of the river.

Doc supervised the unloading of his horse and looked about for some advice on the trails he should take if he hoped to intercept Raider and the gang he was still chasing.

"Damned if I'd know," one of the loafers told him. "Furthest I've been from the tracks is the crapper out back of Nellie Armitage's whorehouse."

The response of other men he talked with in Buena Vista were similar if less colorful. Some of the men, but by no means all of them, had found cause to visit mining camps high to the west. No one seemed to have knowledge of the country or conditions to the east and south.

"What I'd say you should ought to do," one man finally ventured, "is go down to Johnson Village. That's where the Denver, South Park, an' Pacific crosses the river an' joins up with the Denver an' Rio Grande. They got a bridge down there. An' somebody might know something 'bout that part of the country. But mind you be careful down there, mister. No offense, but you look like a gennulmun an' not some rough-an'-tumble kind of fella. And there're some mean sons of bitches down to Johnson Village. Not like the class of folks we got here. So watch yourself, if you know what I mean."

"Thank you." Doc took no offense at all from the man's comments. He was, after all, only trying to be helpful.

Johnson Village was only a half hour's ride to the south along the west bank of the Arkansas. The bridge across the river at this point was only the narrow-gauge railroad span with some extra planking thrown down to provide a more or less solid surface for foot traffic. The bridge was wide enough that a narrow wagon *might* have been able to negotiate the crossing—if the driver was careful, the horses not balky, and no train came along to catch the outfit in the middle of the span. Weatherbee took the precaution of walking the hired horse across. He did not know the animal well enough to trust it, and the river below was white-foamed and swift, hardly ideal for a swim.

A group of bearded and very obviously unbathed men were lounging in the thin sunshine outside a small store on the outskirts of the village. They spat tobacco juice and watched as the nattily dressed Weatherbee approached them.

"Good afternoon, gentlemen." Doc touched the brim of his bowler in greeting. "Could any of you point me toward the trails leading southeast? Toward Texas Creek, say?"

There were five idlers in the group. Four of them turned to stare at the fifth man, a large and rather filthy creature who sat in the center of the group. The fifth man gave Weatherbee a stare that he probably meant to be intimidating, then before he responded glanced toward his friends and gave them a wink.

"Seen you walk that horse o' yorn acrost the bridge. Too scairt to ride, huh?"

"That's right," Doc said agreeably. "Or too intelligent to pursue foolish risks. Sometimes the ignorant have difficulty differentiating between the two." He was smiling.

The big man chewed on that for a moment.

"Your dandy's a smartass, Bill," one of the other loafers put in.

"Called you ignorant, Bill," another prompted. It was plain that the men would welcome the diversion of a fight.

As long, Doc suspected, as they were not required to participate in it.

"What you oughta do, Bill, is whip his smart ass for him."

"Or don't you think you can?" That crack brought a round of laughter from the group, the loudest laugh coming from Bill.

Doc considered simply turning away from them. But he suspected that would do no good now. Now that they had started they would probably just want to pursue him and push the matter further once they thought they had him on the run. Besides, he still needed to know how to find the trailhead.

"You haven't answered my question," Doc said softly. "Or are you just another depot loafer frightened of being far from a roof and a saloon?"

Bill laughed loud and long at that notion. "Shit, little fella, I been all over this country. Worked down to Fisher, Bowdrie, Halleluia, all them camps. Till they played out. There ain't shit down that way now but bones an' fallin'-down shacks an' big holes in the ground where honest men used to work. Yeah, I know that country. But why'd I want to tell you about it?"

"Because I asked politely."

"Don't tell him nothin', Bill."

"'Less he earns it."

"Yeah, Bill, make the dandy earn it."

"Tell him if'n he can whip you.'

"Yeah, Bill, if he whups you."

The whole group broke up in laughter.

Weatherbee continued to smile gently.

"Aw, I don' know, boys. Wouldn't hardly be fair, him bein' so puny.'

Doc's strength was not particularly apparent. The blond Pinkerton was a bit on the soft side, to all appearances, but he had the speed and the stamina of a bullwhip. His abilities were something he did not choose to flaunt.

"You ain't scared of this city feller, are you, Bill?" one of the loafers asked. And quickly there was more of the same from the rest of them. Doc was aware that these unpleasant loafers were quite willing to turn on their companion, and so apparently was Bill. The big man looked around at the others, and Doc thought there was a certain amount of nervousness in his eyes.

"I have an even better idea," Doc said, still smiling. "As Bill says, we all know that he could thrash me. But could any two of you other, uh, gentlemen?" The smile remained unchanged.

"Huh?"

"You." Doc pointed. "And you. You both seem willing enough to egg on a man who is better than either of you," he nodded toward Bill. "But you are willing to defend the price of my information?"

"I don' know—"

"I thought so," Doc snapped. He gave the two a thin-lipped smile and turned again to Bill. "Might I ask you again, sir, how to gain the trail leading to, uh, Halleluia and points beyond?"

Bill looked perfectly willing to answer now, but his friends acted first. One of the two Doc had pointed toward let out a bellow and charged forward. Two of the others were close behind.

Weatherbee let go of the reins of the horse he had been leading and stepped out of the way. He allowed his left foot to remain planted where it had been, though, and the idler tripped over it and sprawled face down in the dirt.

A second man, close behind the first, threw a wide, looping punch that could have broken Doc's jaw if it had landed. It did not. Weatherbee ducked under it and jabbed a short, vicious combination of lefts and rights into the man's solar plexus. The man turned away, gagging, and went down to his knees in a quick search for suddenly missing breath.

The third stopped. His expression said that things were not going quite the way they were supposed to.

A wild punch from behind banged off the back of Doc's skull, knocking his bowler flying and bringing a sharp sting to his scalp. The first man was back on his feet and attacking once again.

Doc whirled, used his left forearm to flick another

punch harmlessly aside, and jabbed a snake-swift strike into the cartilage of the first man's throat with his extended knuckles. At three-to-one odds Doc was not interested in playing by the Marquis of Queensberry rules.

The man turned pale, spun away, and bent over to vomit up the drinks he had had during the day.

"Now," Doc said mildly, "your turn." He smiled at the third man, who was the only one of the three combatants left who might have been able to continue the fight.

"Shit, uh..." The third man glanced nervously back toward Bill and the last loafer, then turned and scuttled quickly down the street without once looking back.

Bill grinned and gave Doc a wink, then bent and picked up Doc's hat from the dusty street. He straightened the crumpled brim and brushed off the crown before he handed it back. "You was asking, Mister?"

"Yes. About that trail."

The other two men who had been inclined to fight climbed painfully to their feet and began to wobble off in the wake of the third fellow, each of them helping to support the other.

"C'mon, mister. I'll show you the way," Bill said.

"That is very kind of you, sir. Thank you."

"Anytime, mister." Bill started to chuckle. And after a few moments Weatherbee did too.

CHAPTER TWENTY-EIGHT

"Aw, *shit!*"

Raider hurriedly pulled the horse to a stop and dropped out of the saddle. The big sorrel tried to pull away from him, hopping sideways on three legs with its off rear hoof held gingerly clear of the stony ground.

Raider ducked under the animal's neck and, still holding the end of the reins, lifted the foot. The horse had all of a sudden begun to limp quite badly, and now it was unwilling to put any weight at all on the hoof.

The shoe was well and properly set. The nails were all in place and correctly crimped. Raider dug his folding knife out of his pocket and used it to clean away the bits of impacted gravel and turf that had collected between the frog and shoe.

What he saw there made him go white and fury.

Those bastards!

There, close to the steel of the shoe, almost too small and too dirt-encrusted to see, was the head of a nail.

It was damn near impossible for the horse to have picked up a fallen nail by accident in such a spot.

The horse had been deliberately sored.

The nail had been partially driven into the tender foot and then left there with the head exposed. It took only time and a few miles of travel before the repeated impact from bits of rock and gravel drove the nail deep into the foot itself.

If the nail was long enough—and Raider had the sickening feeling that it would be—the horse would be lame for weeks, possibly even months, before it would fully recover from an injury like that.

"Whoa, boy. It's all right. You're gonna be all right now," he crooned softly to the animal. He used the blade of the knife to slowly and gently begin prizing the nail out of the horny hoof material. It was difficult work because the cut horseshoe nail that had been used had a sloping shoulder rather than a flat head, and the blade of the knife kept slipping.

As careful and gentle as he was with the horse, though, inside Raider remained in a cold fury.

He kept thinking back to the encounter with the cowboy.

The man had been hunkered beside his campfire. Nowhere close to the pair of horses he had tethered beside the stream.

The cowboy had never once approached the animals, not even after he had made the trade for Raider's horse. And Raider's money.

Raider had been the only one who came near the sorrel then, when he switched his saddle and gear from the rented horse to this one.

So that nail had been emplaced and the soring done before Raider ever came over that switchback and saw the man and horses below him.

It had been done ahead of time.

Those sons of bitches had planned it. They had deliberately provided Raider with a sored horse.

Come to think of it, damn it, there had been two horses there. Likely both of them had been nail-sored. Because the pricks would not have known that Doc Weatherbee wasn't still on the chase.

They'd been prepared for him again. They'd come out on top again.

All this while Raider was thinking he was getting it over on them finally, and the whole time they were in control.

Jesus!

His thoughts were furious but his hands were gentle as

he finally pulled the nail out far enough that he could get a good grip on it and yank it free.

The last shred of hope was gone when he saw how long the nail was.

The steel would have penetrated far into the quick inside the tough covering of the sorrel's foot.

The animal would be damned lucky if it wasn't permanently ruined.

And Raider...

He looked ahead, up the trail the gang had taken. The trail that now seemed suspiciously easy to follow.

Bastards!

Which was hardly news.

He looked back the way he had come. He had made—it took him a moment to think back and try to work it out—he had come probably seven miles since swapping horses with the cowboy.

Seven miles. Call that three hours of walking if he led the limping, virtually three-legged horse with him.

Call it two hours if he he left the horse here and went on on foot. And that would be if he hurried. It would have been less time on flat ground. But this country here was anything but flat. The uphills would turn a man's lungs to fire. The downhills would beat his legs to jelly. Walking these trails would be a bitch.

But, damn it, the only choices Raider had were to walk after the gang and continue the chase on foot, give up the chase and lead the lame horse out, or go back and find that sneaky SOB of a cowboy. The asshole had to have some horse available, if only the half-shot mount Raider had left there for him to let rest up.

None of those choices was worth a damn, but Raider had no trouble choosing among them.

He stripped his gear from the lame sorrel and turned the animal loose.

There was no sense in being encumbered with his saddle and bags. He could come back for those.

He draped the bridle over his shoulder, plucked his Winchester out of its scabbard, and set out at a fast, angry pace back toward that sorry son of a bitch of a cowboy and whatever trouble that lowlife wanted to offer.

And the way Raider felt right now, the more trouble the cowboy wanted, the better.

CHAPTER TWENTY-NINE

Doc topped out on one of the innumerable low peaks and stopped to let the horses rest. Almost as an afterthought back at Johnson Village he had picked up another horse on the theory that when he did find Raider the sap was likely to need a fresh mount. And since he had an extra horse anyway he decided to load it with supplies and a small tent. Roughing it when necessary was one thing, voluntary masochism another; given a choice Doc preferred his comforts.

The outfitter back in Johnson Village had also talked him into buying some cold weather gear. "Just in case," the man had advised. "You see them clouds the other side of Mount Antero? Could mean nothing but shade. Or this time of year they could be full of snow just as easy. Man never knows in this country. Only weeks of the year that I haven't seen snow yet is the last week in July and the first one of August. And I wouldn't take bets that it won't snow one of them weeks come next summer. So if you want my advice, and it don't make any nevermind to me either way you want to go, you'll be prepared for whatever the sky throws at you."

Doc had taken the man's advice.

The country that lay in front of him now was not so spectacular as much he had seen. To the west of the Arkansas the mountains were truly majestic, soaring to heights of better than 14,000 feet for range after long range. Here the peaks were picayune in comparison, rarely rising past 10,000 feet or so, certainly never reaching above timberline.

But Lord, there were a lot of them. One after another in a poorly defined jumble, with the creeks and watersheds crisscrossing willy-nilly in no pattern Doc could discern.

And the slopes between them were raw and breathlessly steep.

It was country that would be hell to get lost in, and if it hadn't been for the long-unused trail that Bill had pointed out for him, Doc would have despaired of ever finding his way. As it was, though, he had every hope of being able to intercept the gang. According to Bill this was the only free passage that a sane man was apt to take, and unless the men were natives to the area they would be virtually forced to follow the marked route through the low mountains.

Doc stepped off his horse and loosened his cinches, then pulled his brass telescope from his saddlebags and sat on a convenient boulder to look over the country that lay below him.

He didn't really expect to make contact with the gang quite yet, but he wasn't foolish enough to take that for granted. Weatherbee was a firm believer in the old adage about an ounce of prevention being better than a pound of cure.

He was in no hurry, though. He laid the opened telescope in his lap and lighted a cheroot, enjoying those first few puffs before he turned his attention to the zigzag cut of the trail on the mountainside below his feet. Behind him the horses blew and shook themselves, then bent to crop noisily at the sparse brown grasses that grew here.

The eyepiece of the telescope brought the valley beneath him snapping up toward his feet. Or so it appeared, in any event.

Doc jammed the Old Virginia between his teeth and swept the lens back and forth over the visible terrain in a slow, slow pattern.

Nothing. As best he could tell from here this trail might not have been used for months. Perhaps for years. Certainly no tracks had been left on it since the past rains, and there was no telling how long that might have been. A few scrapes left by the passage of coyotes or big cats. Now and then the delicate, heart-shaped imprint of a mule deer.

Once the larger, bolder print of a mature elk. That was all he had seen since he gained the trail and left the Arkansas out of view to his rear. The story seemed to be very much the same on the path he was able to follow down into the valley.

He looked as well across to the next slope he would have to climb, easily picking out the thin, artificial line of the trail as it climbed back and forth along the face of the low mountain. Nothing moved over there, and from this distance and this angle it would have been impossible for him to look for prints in the hard, sunbaked earth.

He dropped the objective lens toward the narrow floor of the valley. Despite the lateness of the season there was still a thin trickle of live water running between the rocks and what would be a sizable stream during the melt. The valley was choked with scrub oak, already past its brilliant red stage to the drab, dull browns of winter, and with the bare stems of lesser brush.

Except for the sparkle of the moving water reflecting sunlight there seemed to be no movement there either. Doc laid the brass barrel down in his lap and puffed with some contentment on his cheroot. The afternoon sun felt warm on his cheek, and he was half tempted to drowse while the horses rested.

A flicker of motion deep in the scrub caught his eye. It was too far away for him to see with the naked eye, so he raised the telescope again and searched back and forth until he found the spot he wanted.

It was only a deer down there. A doe. He looked again and saw the half-grown fawn that was at her side. The little one would stick with its dam for another year before she pushed it out on its own.

Doc enjoyed watching wildlife, particularly undisturbed animals that had no idea there were humans near. He kept the glass trained on the doe, enjoying the fluid, easy motion of it, the alert tilt of its ears and the big, gentle eyes that seemed never to lose their wariness. He puffed on his cheroot and watched as the fawn, which would already have been weaned, tried to steal a snack from its mother's bag and was pushed rudely aside.

Doc chuckled at the sight.

But the sound halted in his throat and he leaned forward as both doe and fawn unexpectedly crouched and with a flick of their tails leaped wildly away.

Where the two deer had just stood the telescope brought close the sight of a wooden shaft slashing through the recently vacated air.

The deer were gone. In their place, upright in the soil and quivering from the impact, stood a peeled length of bare wood.

A spear? Who in these modern times would be trying to hunt game with a spear? And why? Even the poorest Indians—and there should be no Indians within miles of here anyway—had firearms nowadays.

Was it really a spear?

Doc looked again. The shaft remained where he had last seen it, unmistakably a wooden spear.

Even as he watched, a rather small and slender arm slipped out from the covering screen of brown, dried oak leaves to pluck the spear from the ground and withdraw it from his sight.

Someone was down there, and it sure as hell looked like that someone was in need of help.

Weatherbee crushed his cheroot out on the boulder and hurried back to his horses.

CHAPTER THIRTY

Raider left the trail well above the point where it reached more or less level ground and slid as silently as he could down into the thin, nearly leafless brush at the bottom of the gulch. There was no sign of the damned cowboy, but he was not going to take any more chances.

The cowboy's campfire had been extinguished. The man had taken the bother to dowse it with water before he left, Raider saw as he came closer and stepped over the slender rill of sluggish water that was flowing in the center of the creekbed.

There was no sign of the man, though, nor of the horses.

Damn it.

No sign of much of anything except the cold, soggy ashes where the fire had been and some manure where the horses had rested. "Damn it," Raider repeated, this time aloud. He straightened from the crouch he had been in and allowed the Winchester to fall to arm's length at his side.

Where . . . ?

The gravel near his feet erupted into a sudden fanlike spray that rattled against his boot tops, and a moment later he heard the flat, ugly sound of a gunshot coming from above and to his rear.

By then Raider was already in motion, diving toward the scanty protection of the brush in front of him.

Another shot sounded from somewhere on the slope, and this time he could see the thin wisp of white powder smoke despite the distraction of flung gravel stinging his chest and forearms. He was not nearly as well hidden as he needed to be. He scuttled backward on hands and knees.

The rifle fired again—he was sure it was a rifle because of the sparseness of the smoke; a revolver or pistol with its shorter barrel emitted much more gunsmoke than a rifle or carbine—and again Raider was sprayed with gravel. The gunman had him spotted all too well.

Raider came to his knees and triggered a response toward the powder smoke. His slug whined off a boulder on the mountainside and sped harmlessly away.

This time it was a second rifle that answered, from someplace to the left, and yet again Raider felt the painful sting of gravel peppering his jeans.

His position was beginning to look damn well unhealthy. Those riflemen could not keep on missing forever.

He retreated, on his feet now and darting from tree trunk to tree trunk up the course of the creekbed, stopping now and then to answer the gang's rifles with his own but knowing good and well that the two riflemen were much too well protected for him to have much hope of hitting them.

And nearly every time he paused he was pelted with sharp bits of gravel.

The riflemen were shooting low. If they ever got the range, though, he would be in deep shit.

The thin copse of aspen ended and with it Raider's shelter, meager though it had been.

In front of him now was another long, narrow pocket of bare rock, loose gravel, and clumps of brown grass. Absolutely nothing that would afford any protection for more than a hundred yards up the creek toward a tangle of driftwood left by last year's runoff.

Across the creek and much closer to the edge of the aspen grove there was the dark, gaping mouth of a tunnel. Probably an abandoned mine or prospect hole.

He was tempted to run for it.

If the hole was a shaft running deep into the rock it would be a haven of safety.

But if the damned thing was only a shallow prospect hole it would be a death trap. Inside a shallow pocket of hard rock, a man would be chopped to pieces by slugs fired at random into the mouth of the hole and allowed to wickedly ricochet back and forth until they found flesh to lodge in.

Shit, Raider thought. But the temptation was there.

If he tried to cross that long stretch of open ground he wouldn't have a chance.

One of the rifles boomed high above him, and he felt the sting of the gravel against his legs.

The other weapon fired, and this time the slug plunked with a heavy, hollow sound into the trunk of the aspen Raider was leaning against. The bullet thumped home within inches of his right ear. The riflemen were beginning to get the damned range.

That knowledge more than the gunfire itself was enough to galvanize Raider into sudden motion.

Crouching low, he dashed forward, away from the protection of the aspen trunks, up the narrow gulch. He took four long, running strides, then darted to the side, angling for the dark, empty mouth of the tunnel.

The sonuvabitch *had* to be a tunnel. He couldn't even consider the possibility that it might be only a shallow exploration hole.

A rifle boomed high above, and gravel spat forward from a spot in front of Raider and to his left. He angled right again, heading openly now for the shaft.

Two more steps and he leaped forward, jumping high and fast, crossing the creek and the whole damned, stony creekbed in one long stride, stumbling, righting himself, racing forward.

A slug spanged nastily into the rock wall in front of him, sending rock chips into the air and leaving behind a silvery stain of friction-melted lead.

Raider threw himself forward into the tunnel, rolled, and came to his knees. He whirled around and sent a string of three blind shots out of the tunnel mouth, then turned and began inching along the tunnel.

If it was deep enough...

It was. Sixty, seventy feet in from the mouth the shaft angled rather sharply upward, probably the result of some long-gone miner following a lead of color, and then dropped back down again toward the dark bowels of the earth.

There was no light this far back. But neither were there any bullets.

Raider could hear continued shooting from outside the mouth of the shaft, but there was no sizzling, bumblebee drone of ricocheting lead. No slugs came anywhere close to him. He turned and moved back toward the mouth just far enough to be able to get some benefit from the small amount of light that was able to penetrate, just far back enough to remain safe from the shooting.

The bastards might think they had him now, but they'd gone and grabbed a tiger by the tail.

Raider didn't intend to be taken easily.

CHAPTER THIRTY-ONE

If he hadn't *known* there was someone down there—if he hadn't seen for himself that hand come out of the brush and grab up the spear—Doc would never have found her. In fact, for quite a little while there he was beginning to doubt his own senses and conclude that he had imagined what he in fact had seen.

Eventually, though, he did find her. A young woman. Hiding under the overhang of a large rock with gravel and bits of ground litter drawn hastily over the tiny opening from an arm's-length distance between stone and soil.

He had noticed and rejected looking there at least half a dozen times earlier because of the sheer impossibility of a human form fitting into that narrow space.

Yet there she was.

When the woman—girl, really—finally betrayed herself with an indrawn gasp of fear, Doc hunkered close to the opening and coaxed her out.

"It's all right," he kept insisting. "You're hungry. I have food. Come out and let me help you."

Eventually, slowly and as timidly as a rabbit venturing from its burrow, the girl emerged. She pushed the trash away from the mouth of the burrow she had created for herself and squeezed out into the clear light of day.

She was hardly a comely sight. Small and frail, no larger than a half-grown girl, she was filthy dirty and her hair unkempt.

Hair, eyes, and skin were dark. It took Weatherbee several close looks before he concluded that she was probably of Indian ancestry rather than Hispanic.

Her dress was made of leather, the toughness of the material probably the only reason the garment retained any form that was recognizable. Cloth would have been torn to rags from the rough use the leather had received. There were no fringes or decorations on it, though, to give him a hint at the tribe she must have come here.

The most remarkable—and alarming—thing about her was the clot of dried mud and small fibers that had been plastered thick on both sides of her nose.

It took Doc a moment to realize what that was. It was a mixture of mud and spider web, kneaded together to make a poultice. The healing mixture had been applied to wounds on both sides of her nose.

Then it clicked, and he understood. The woman was an outcast from her tribe. She had been judged an adulteress, and both her nostrils had been slit. It was a common enough form of punishment among the northern tribes for that crime. Some tribes went so far as to cut the offending woman's nose completely away to mark her forever. Other tribes, of course, had no concept of fidelity and simply didn't give a damn who their women slept with.

"You'll be all right now," Doc said gently. Whoever this young woman was and whatever she may have done in the past, she was now a human being in need, and he was in a position to help her. He could not do less.

"You'll be all right now. I have some jerky in my packs. We'll get you some of that to start on and put a fire together to get some proper food into you." His voice was gentle and soothing in an attempt to offset the nervousness he could see in her posture and in the quick darting of her large eyes.

She obviously understood English. But instead of moving toward the packhorse and the promised jerky, she knelt and began to assemble small pieces of dry wood to make a fire. She took a bit of native flint from a pouch at her waist and, using an old-fashioned fire steel, she had a fire alight almost as quickly as he could have done it with modern sulphur matches. Weatherbee went himself to unload the packhorse. It was almost time for a dinner stop anyway.

The girl ate quickly and very, very little. She must have been a long time without food for her to act that way, Doc realized.

Only later, with her shrunken stomach groaningly full, did he try to talk to her again.

"Do you feel better now?"

She nodded.

"Do you have . . . any place to go? People to take you in?"

She shook her head. Whoever she was and wherever she had come from, she was not exactly big on conversation.

"Do you want to tell me about it?"

She shrugged and seemed to think about that for a moment. Finally she spoke for the first time. "I was Ute. But no more."

That explained much, then. This country had been the ancestral wintering grounds of the Ute nation. But that was before gold was found and South Park, not too many miles to the north, became white man's territory. Now the Utes were all confined on a reservation in the far southwestern corner of Colorado. Apparently this girl—a gap at the front of her dress kept proving to him that she was in fact a woman, but her diminutive size and shy manner insisted that he think of her as a girl—had returned to a place of happier memories after her banishment.

She touched the mud that was still packed on her nose, and Doc nodded his understanding. He did not want to cause her the pain of having to explain that.

"It's all right," he said. "You are going to be fine now."

The girl nodded again, the gratitude she did not express in words showing in her eyes and in her expression.

"I can . . . I don't know. I can't take you in to town now. There's something I have to do first. But maybe later I could take you someplace, find you a job, something. You can't try to live alone like this. You would surely starve without weapons to hunt with or help if you got hurt."

The girl looked sad at the thought. But he thought she seemed resigned to his suggestion too.

Without speaking again she began to gather up the tin

plates and cookware he had used in their cooking. She carried them to the stream and washed them.

Then with no hint of modesty she pulled off the leather dress—it was her only garment, he quickly discovered—and bathed herself as well.

She was even thinner than he had realized. Her ribs were boldly visible under a taut layer of dark skin, and her breasts, which would have been none too large to begin with, sagged loosely from the loss of body fats. There was not a spare ounce anywhere on her that he could see. And he had no difficulty seeing all of her. Her thighs barely swelled, leaving a wide embarrassingly appealing gap between them for the thick bush of dark hair at her crotch.

Doc looked away and tried to concentrate on extinguishing the fire. It would not do to show any smoke if the gang members were anywhere near already. He doubted that they were yet, but at least that gave him an excuse for thinking about something other than the naked Indian girl who was washing herself so carefully in the cold creek water.

Doc had the distinct impression that she was preparing herself for an expression of gratitude somewhat more substantial than a simple thank-you.

CHAPTER THIRTY-TWO

Night. It wouldn't be long now. It would be Raider's best chance to get out of the tunnel, which was beginning now to seem as much trap as protection. Every time he moved, every time he kicked a rock or made any kind of damned noise, the yahoos outside went to shooting again. If nothing else they were well supplied with ammunition.

Well supplied, Raider thought with a bitter grunt. He could use some supply himself about now. He'd been holed up inside the old mine tunnel for the better part of the afternoon, and it had been pressed on him long since that he hadn't had much to eat during the day. And all of his supplies were back where he had cached his saddle and other gear while he walked back to have words with that cowboy.

The simple truth was that the bastards had been ahead of him again, and now it looked like he was well and thoroughly stuck where he was.

They couldn't get in at him. But then he couldn't get out to them either. It was a standoff, but in the long haul he would be the one holding the short, shitty end of the proverbial stick because they could get to all the food and water they needed while he was stuck here in an empty tunnel.

Just how empty he really did not know yet, though, because most of his time had been spent sitting well back from the tunnel mouth with the Winchester over his knees, waiting for one of them to get foolish enough to come in after him. So far none of them had.

While he still had a little daylight left, actually stronger now that the sun had angled lower so as to reach deeper inside the shaft, it was time for him to do some looking. He propped the Winchester against the rock wall and stood, his joints creaking after more than an hour of inactivity.

When he moved he kicked a stone, sending it pinging against the steel of a tram rail that once would have been used by the ore carts. The sound was enough to draw a fresh burst of gunfire from outside the tunnel mouth.

The sound enveloped him, and slugs whined and howled near the front of the shaft, but nothing came near him. The shocks of concussion were enough to plug his ears and bring rock dust spilling down onto his shoulders from the roof, but they did no damage. Interesting, though, that the men with the guns must have moved closer to the mouth. That was going to make it harder for him to slip out come dark.

He let the sound of their gunfire cover his movements and retreated deeper inside the tunnel. It was as dark as the pits of hell once he got past the hump, and he had to feel his way along slowly.

This wasn't going to do much, he realized, and he had only a few matches with him.

He had no means to make a torch for himself, but he had something almost as good. Raider dropped to his hands and knees and felt between the twin, narrow rails where the carts had been pulled. He easily found what he needed. Ancient, dried-out clumps of burro shit. He assembled all he could find into a conical pile and applied a match to the dry dung.

It was as good as buffalo chips for fuel. The stuff took flame and flared. The light was weak, manure giving off more heat than live flame, but it was enough to let him see. He added the spent match to his fire and looked around for more mature to pile onto the flame.

After a moment he began to grin.

The miners who had worked this tunnel knew then what he was discovering now—that here was where they ran out of light. And they'd been prepared for it.

A shallow niche had been blown out of the side wall not ten feet from where Raider was. Old powder boxes were piled there.

Raider had no reason to believe that the boxes would still hold giant powder, although it would be nice to be able to find the means to build a bomb and maybe help get him out of here. But the wood would be a damned welcome addition to his fire if he broke the boxes up and used the slats for fuel.

He paused for a moment, listening for activity out toward the tunnel mouth. He could hear nothing. Reassured for the moment, he took down the topmost box and stomped it under his boot heel, breaking the wooden joints and scattering splintered slats on the floor. He added those to the fire and took up the second box.

There were four boxes in all, one of them smaller than the others and marked as having contained Hayworth's Patented Blasting Caps, No. 4.

Raider broke up the powder boxes and piled the wood from them near the fire. He was wondering if he could somehow make use of the fuel to make a torch of sorts that would allow him to explore deeper into the tunnel. Somewhere back there, if the shaft ran deep enough, there might be an air vent or vertical shaft that would give him an alternate way out.

He picked up the small box. It was much heavier than it looked. Or should have been.

The lid was a flat slab of wood that rode inside morticed grooves. He pulled it aside.

Shee-it, he thought with satisfaction. It was some kind of emergency kit that must have been left behind by mistake.

There was a rusty cap-lamp inside and a small tin of carbide to fire it. Some flat cans of sardines. Four of those. A block of matches. Half a dozen candles. Two rolls of linen bandage wrappings.

And best of all there was a quart-sized glass jar with a rusted lid. The jar held a clear liquid that almost had to be water.

Seeing it, Raider's throat constricted and his saliva began to run freely. He had been unwilling to admit to himself just how dry he was getting.

With this, hell, he could wait it out this whole first night, when they would be expecting him to try to break out, and go tomorrow night when the guards outside should be getting lazy in their attentions.

Hell, yes.

Grinning, Raider twisted the lid off the jar and smelled of the contents.

It was water, all right. It had a musty, sour odor to it. But then there was no telling how long it might have been sealed up and forgotten in the box.

One can of sardines tonight, he decided, and another in the morning. And a good swallow of the water with each can. The jar held about a quart, he judged. It would be enough.

Grinning, he used his knife to open the first can of sardines and wolfed them down, licking up every last bit of the oil the fishes had been packed in. The oil was strength in liquid form, and he wanted to waste none of it.

Finally the treat he had been saving until last.

He took a deep swallow of the water, holding it in his mouth to savor it, allowing it to trickle at last down his throat.

Those bastards were *not* going to get him, Raider swore to himself.

He carefully screwed the lid back onto the jar of water and walked back to the fire.

The low flame looked a bit fuzzy, he noticed. He would have to do something about that.

Funny, though. The fire was burning high enough. It just looked fuzzy.

For that matter, so did the damn walls.

He blinked rapidly, trying to clear his vision, which all of a sudden seemed cloudy.

Smoke from the fire, he told himself. That was all it was. Just smoke filling the tunnel.

He blinked again and realized with a start that he was no

longer walking toward the fire. Somehow he'd come to be leaning against the wall. The rock at his side felt cool and refreshing.

He tried to take a step forward, staggered, and felt himself slumping down on his knees instead.

There was a low, droning buzz inside his head. That was where the smoke was, then. It wasn't inside the tunnel at all. It was inside his head.

The thought of smoke swirling and filling an empty cavity inside his skull sent Raider into a spasm of great good humor. He heard himself laugh.

He blinked again. There was something...not quite *right* about this. He was not sure just what it was that failed to be right. But there was something.

Not that it really mattered all that much.

He yawned and chuckled.

There was that smoke again. It was behind his eyes this time, not in front of them.

It really made the inside of the cave—tunnel, he corrected—it really made the inside of the cave rather pretty.

It was like there was a pink haze softening the outlines of everything and making them much more attractive than the plain old gray he had seen before.

Smiling, quite content with the world, Raider's chin slumped down toward his chest.

He drifted away into a deep, drug-induced sleep.

After a few minutes he began to snore.

CHAPTER THIRTY-THREE

Weatherbee woke to the warm, willing presence of the girl. Sometime during the last minute of his sleep he had become aware of her nearness, responded to it, and now had a raging erection. The girl—she had told him her name; it was some unpronounceable combination of sounds that might have been mistaken for a prolonged belch but could be shortened to Jane—felt his need and accommodated it.

Minutes later, his breathing returning to normal, Doc pulled back the covers they had shared through the night and sat upright.

During the night the air had become noticeably colder. It chilled his bare, sweat-sheened chest and sent him hurrying into his clothing.

Jane seemed not to notice the cold. She raised her face toward the gray clouds that were scudding overhead and sniffed nosily. "Storm," she said. "Very bad."

"Too early in the season for that," Doc said. But the comment was more wish than conviction.

The girl shrugged, obviously not wanting to disagree with him in so many words but disagreeing nonetheless, and went to the creek. She bathed in the icy water, dried herself with handfuls of brown grass pulled from the bank, and dressed in the single thin garment she owned.

She had to be cold—Weatherbee still was in spite of the heavy, fleece-lined coat he had purchased at Johnson Village—but she refused to show any discomfort. He broke open one of the packs and handed her the coat he had brought for Raider. The sheepskin, cut to fit a man of

Raider's size, hung nearly to her knees and left her hands somewhere near elbow level but should keep her warm. Her feet were still bare, so Doc found several pairs of extra woolen socks to take care of that end of things. It was the best he could manage without turning back.

"If you want," he said, "I can give you some money. You know the way out? You could go out alone. I don't have much money with me, but it would give you a start somewhere."

The girl shook her head and knelt to start their breakfast fire.

"Why?"

She did not bother to answer. She had to bend very low to shield her tinder from a rising wind, but she quickly had bright flame licking at the kindling she added. Within minutes she had a roaring fire crackling and flaring. Doc handed her a slab of bacon and his knife and went to see to the horses.

She was an odd one, he thought. Quiet and agreeable enough in most ways. But a bit off-putting from that lump of mud and spiderweb on her nose.

He looked toward the sky as he led first one horse and then the other to the creek to drink.

He hated to admit it, but Jane might have been right about the weather. It felt colder than ever now with the wind continuing to rise.

And down at the west end of the narrow valley he could see a thin white veil of light snow moving toward them. He shivered.

Whatever Raider was up to, wherever he and the gang were right now, Raider was not prepared for this.

Doc sent a silent thank-you back toward the Johnson Village outfitter who had talked him into the extra purchases. He pulled his coat collar high around his neck and joined the girl at the fire. A hot breakfast was going to feel almighty good in his stomach today.

CHAPTER THIRTY-FOUR

Son of a bitch but the pounding at his temples was fixing to bust right through his skull. Had to, because nothing could withstand that kind of thumping for very long.

Raider was conscious first of the drums that were beating inside his head. Then of the sharp pains that cut across his body about waist level. Finally of the difficulty he was having trying to breathe.

It took him a while of woozy half-consciousness before he could work out that he was no longer inside the mine shaft. He was outdoors. Hands and feet tied. Draped across the damn well unyielding seat of a saddle and being taken somewhere.

It was only then that he realized how miserably cold he was to. After that he began to shiver until his teeth were chattering.

Raider tried to look around. From the position they had placed him in all he could see was the passage of reddish yellow gravel a few feet over his head. Or under it. It took him a while to decide which. Finally he looked forward, in the direction the horse was traveling, and became properly oriented between the earth and the sky.

There were three men riding ahead of him, one of them the "cowboy" he had gotten the sored horse from and another pair behind. He recognized every one of the sons of bitches.

The effects of the drug were beginning to wear off now, and he was able to think again with some degree of clarity.

The bastards had been ahead of his thinking yet again.

No old-timey miner had forgotten that emergency kit. The damned gang had planted it there waiting for him, then deliberately drove him into the mine tunnel for refuge.

That knowledge did nothing to help the way he was feeling. He'd felt dumb enough before. Now he was beginning to think of himself as a prime asshole to have let them take him so damned easy.

One good thing. If that damned Weatherbee had been along, he would have been taken in just as bad. Raider was sure of that. Oddly, that made him feel not the least bit better than he had. His own body weight was cutting unnaturally against the seat of the hard saddle and making him hurt in every nerve ending. Every step the damn horse took sent fresh waves of pain through him, and it was still almost impossible for him to breathe.

This whole thing was a bitch of the first water.

Water. He grunted. That had to be what did the trick for them. The stuff hadn't smelled from being old. It smelled from whatever they'd put in it to knock him out like that.

Bastards, he mouthed silently.

Come to think of it, there was no reason he had to be quiet about this.

"Bastards," he shouted at them.

The riders ignored him.

The six-horse cavalcade wound up a series of switchbacks, crossed from one drainage into another, and worked its way slowly back down again. Raider cussed the riders just about every other step of the way. *Every* step of it pounded the leather into his belly and hurt all the way down to his toenails.

The men didn't bother to answer him. Not once.

Now that he was fully awake—a mixed blessing—Raider could see the trail that lay before them.

There was a split at the bottom of the hill, another narrow branch of long unused trail coming in from the right and joining with the one they were following. The tail of the Y led up the gulch and over a low pass that Raider could see ahead of them.

The bearded prick in the lead seemed to know where he was going. He kept the pace steady and much faster than

Raider would have liked. Except that going faster would maybe get him off this damned animal that much quicker.

They climbed over the low pass and dropped down into yet another gulch.

This one had to be their destination, Raider saw. It wasn't much for big, but it was hell for rugged.

Sharp mountainside rose all around, broken only by the pass and the thin trace behind them.

There were tunnel openings all over the face that was ahead and to the right, and below those, strung out in a long line that would be just above the water level during the spring melt, probably, there were the tumbledown remains of shacks and shitters. A long-abandoned mining camp, obviously.

There was no sign of life anywhere that Raider could see. Not so much as a magpie or a whistlepig seemed to be moving in the dead camp ahead of them.

They reached the first of the buildings, and the bearded man brought the group to a halt. Raider heard the SOB speak for the first time, his voice a low, sonorous rumble.

"Alonzo, Bray, take *Mister* Raider inside an' see that he's comfortable. The rest of us'll set up in the jail. It's held up the best of what's still standing."

The idea of them using the jail for a headquarters seemed to amuse the rest of the men, and they made joking comments about it as they went about their tasks.

Alonzo and big Bray untied Raider from the horse and untied his feet as well but kept his hands secured. They acted as if they knew what they were doing. Which did not please Raider a whole hell of a lot.

They half carried, half dragged him inside the shack, blocking his view so that he could no longer see what the others were up to. That didn't particularly please him either.

A reception had obviously been readied for him in advance. So it was no accident that the bearded shithead chose this building from the dozen or so that were still mostly intact.

The floor of the building had once been made of wood planking, but now most of that had rotted away to expose the natural floor of sharp gravel and slick rock.

The place was one room. A stub of stovepipe remained in the back wall, although there was no longer a stove in the single room.

A vertical support post had been placed in the center of the room, its base planted deep in solid rock and the top of it spiked firmly to the massive crossbeam above. The post looked solid as hell.

Which was of considerable interest to Raider because a hole had been bored through the post at something over head height—bored recently, too, because he could see fresh wood shavings on the floor below it—and a length of steel chain had been run through the hole and padlocked in place. Locked, not bolted, he noted.

At the free end of the chain there was a set of manacles welded into the last link of the chain.

The manacles were of modern design, Raider saw at a glance. Made of tempered steel and with one of those patented locking designs that was said to be unpickable.

This did not look especially promising, Raider decided.

"Strip," Alonzo said.

"What?"

Alonzo did not bother to answer. Bray did it for him. The big man looped a low, fast fist into Raider's gut, and Raider doubled over.

Raider stripped below his waist, finding the simplest tasks difficult with his wrists bound tight together. But he managed it. It seemed a better idea than absorbing more unnecessary punishment.

When he had gone as far as he could with his hands tied, Alonzo and Bray both drew their revolvers and covered Raider while Bray untied the rope that held his wrists.

"Keep goin'," Alonzo said.

Raider removed his upper clothing and dropped the shirt and jacket on the floor with the rest of his things. His gunbelt was already gone, of course, and his pockets had felt empty when he removed his trousers.

When Raider was completely naked—and damned well cold inside the unheated shack—Bray clamped the manacles around his wrists and checked to make sure both sides had caught and were fully locked.

The short length of chain allowed Raider's hands no lower than his chin.

He was fastened securely to the stout post in the middle of the building, with nothing that he could reach—or even see—to give him hope.

Alonzo grunted his approval of the arrangement, and he and Bray holstered their revolvers and headed toward the doorframe, which was empty of a door now—assuming it had ever had one.

"Hey!" Raider protested.

The two men ignored him. They went out and turned to their right, toward the other standing buildings and the other men in the gang.

Raider was left alone, chained and naked.

He began to shiver and was aware that his teeth had begun to chatter again.

CHAPTER THIRTY-FIVE

Doc hated to admit it, but he was beginning to think the girl had been right. This weather was beginning to look less and less like just an early snow and more and more like a full-fledged storm.

The temperature was continuing to drop at an alarming rate of discomfort, and now the wind was howling around their ears. Or around Doc's ears and where Jane's ears should be. She was bundled so deep into the oversized coat that it was impossible to see any more of her than the shiny black hair on the very top of her head.

If the snow got any heavier, Doc realized, he would be hard put to see the horse she was riding, much less any part of Jane herself. It was getting that thick.

Worse yet, this was not one of the dry, light powder snows of the winter but a freak fall storm with heavy, wet, soggy flakes, some of them lumpy and as big around as nickels.

The danger of that was that moist snow will pack quickly and turn slick. The narrow switchback trail that negotiated a seemingly endless series of ridges and mountaintops could become impossible to traverse.

Doc tucked his chin deep inside the collar of his coat and let his horse pick its own slow way along the path.

They reached the bottom of yet another narrow valley, and the girl kicked her horse up beside Doc's. She materialized at his side like a ghost appearing out of the woodwork. He could not see beyond her and had no idea what their surroundings might be.

ping in behind Jane's. The girl's horse walked slowly, with its head down and rump caked with wet, clinging snow, its tail tucked tight into the crease in its butt.

"I sure as hell hope you know where we're going," Doc muttered. But of course the girl could not hear. Even his own horse did not react to the man's voice, only continued to plod forward one uncomfortable step at a time.

He saw her mouth move, knew she was saying something to him, but he could not make out any of the sounds that came from her mouth. Both of them had to lean sideways in their saddles in order for her to be close enough to be heard.

"Cave," she shouted. "There."

She pointed, but all he could see at the moment was the uncertain curtain of white that was blowing sideways between them and whatever lay behind it.

Doc hesitated for a moment. He stood in his stirrups and peered over his shoulder, hoping for some sign of a break in the weather. But if anything, it only seemed worse behind them.

Raider was somewhere out in the blowing white. Unprepared for it. The gang might be caught in it too, but Doc cared little about that. It was Raider's safety that concerned him. If Raider was trapped out in the open...

Doc shook his head. If Raider was caught in it, even he would be bright enough to take shelter from the elements. Particularly as he had no proper coat or gloves for protection.

And in a way this storm might turn out to be a blessing of sorts.

Once the wind and snow subsided it would be easy to follow the tracks the gang members' horses would leave behind. Even by starlight a newly broken trail could be followed, so Raider would be able to come along at whatever pace his tired horse allowed.

And Doc would be able to sit in comfort and wait for them to show up in front of him. He was positive he was ahead of them. There was no way they could have slipped by him. Not unless they had taken a different route altogether.

"All right," he agreed finally.

He hoped the girl knew where she was. Doc certainly did not. He was blinded by the storm and in completely unfamiliar country. And Jane was right. They had to find a sheltered place where they could ride out the blow. Surely that was what Raider would be doing too.

Doc let the girl take the lead, his horse gratefully drop-

CHAPTER THIRTY-SIX

Raider could think of things that would be more comfortable. Like sitting bareass naked on top of a hot stove. At least then a body would be warm. Miserable, sure, but warm.

He wasn't cold any longer. Hell, he'd passed cold a long time ago. Now there was a serious possibility that he might freeze to death before the bastards got around to whatever it was they had planned for him.

The wind had come up overnight, finding every crack and crevice in the walls—and there were plenty of those—and slicing through to find Raider's entirely exposed flesh. At first it had been like a thousand icicles carved into knife blades, each one of them stabbing into him.

But that was only at first. Now he was so cold all over and all through his body that he could no longer differentiate one patch of chilled flesh from another. All sensation was a long, deep freeze of agony.

And now there was snow along with the wind.

In the gray, watery light of the morning, all too clearly visible through the empty doorway, he had been able to see a few flakes of snow. Then many flakes. And now the world beyond the doorway was a near solid mass of shifting, blowing white.

The snow was driven through the same cracks that admitted the wind. Large, heavy, wet flakes of it that plastered themselves to him only long enough to melt and run in icy streams down his body.

So now he was wet as well as cold.

So far he still had enough body temperature to melt the snow. But the time could come, and all too soon, when his reserves of energy would be used up and the warming flow of living blood would begin to pull back from his extremities as his body tried to protect the valuable central trunk core. Then the melted snow-water would begin to freeze solid on his hands and feet.

Not long after that he would die.

That thought, that knowledge, did not frighten him. It pissed him off.

Thoroughly angry, Raider stamped his bare feet on the rough wooden planks and moved from side to side as far as the confinement of the chain permitted.

His wrists were rubbed raw by the constant strain of being held at head level inside the steel manacles, and his fingers were swollen blue things that more resembled rotten sausages than any part of a human body.

To move was to hurt. But that hardly mattered either. To remain still was to die. And that he refused to do.

He shuffled back and forth, from one limit of the chain to the other, stamping his feet, flexing his knees, straining to form his hands into fists. He had to keep his blood circulating.

As he moved he mouthed curses, directing them toward the men who had done this.

The cocksuckers had some kind of plan for him. That was obvious. If they only wanted to kill him they could have done that easily enough back at the mine when he was drugged and unconscious at their feet.

Instead they had chosen to bring him here, with no small difficulty and danger to themselves because of it.

Surely they had to know that allowing Raider to draw even more breath brought their own lives that much closer to being forfeit. Because if he ever got lose from this chain...

No sense in thinking about that yet, he told himself. Right now the thing was to stay alive.

He kept on shuffling from side to side, ducking and bobbing, stomping his feet.

That was worrisome, though. Last night when he only *thought* he was cold it hurt to stamp his feet on the rough wood. Now he could barely feel the contact. He was aware of it at about calf level, like the soles of his feet had gone to sleep or something. Now he could hear the impact of foot against wood better than he could feel it.

The worry there, aside from frostbite and freezing, was that eventually he would lose control over his feet and then his lower legs, and then he might not be able to maintain his balance. If he could no longer stand he would dangle from his wrists, trapped by that damnable chain. And then he would surely die.

"No!" The single word ripped through his throat and lost itself in the howling moan of the wind.

That hurt too. His throat was dry. They had given him nothing to eat or drink since he woke up trussed like a hog on the back of that horse.

Come to think of it, he really had no idea how long it had been since he passed out inside the old mine or how long they might have let him lie there before someone came into the tunnel to make sure he was safely drugged. He had been assuming that it had only been overnight. For all he knew it could have been several days instead. No wonder he was so damned dry.

And hungry. His gut knotted and churned with unused acids at the thought of food. He needed food. Not only for comfort but for survival. He need the heat of it to fight the cold that was folded around him.

"Bastards!" Raider screamed into the wind.

He continued to shuffle and move. Slow and steady. Back and forth.

"Dancing?" The voice came from the doorway. It was followed by a grunt of laughter. Raider had not seen the man appear at the door. It was Willie, small and unhealthy-looking, with a pointy nose and practically no chin and his eyes set a bit too close together.

"Fuck off," Raider greeted him.

Willie laughed again. "You look kinda pissed, man. Oughta do something about your disposition. I mean, a fella comes by t' do you a favor and you cuss him." Willie shook his head. "That ain't polite. You know?" He laughed again. It sounded like a giggle.

"Fuck you," Raider said.

Willie's eyes narrowed. He wasn't laughing now. "I could take you, Raider. I've heard 'bout how you think you're so tough. But I could take you, mister. On your best damn day I could take you."

"Undo this lock, asshole, and I'll let you prove that."

Willie looked like he wanted to do just that. But after a moment the glare of challenge left his eyes and he became more subdued. "It ain't worth losing all that money," he mumbled.

He came closer to Raider, almost ignoring the taller, much better-looking man now, and reached inside his coat. "Here." He shoved a thick sandwich into Raider's manacled hands, having to lean close and reach high to reach them.

Willie was just about as smart as he looked, Raider thought. Raider could have kicked his cods off for him while he was so close. But that wouldn't have accomplished anything, and right now he wanted that sandwich. Later . . . that would be a different story.

"I want something to drink, too," Raider commanded.

"You get mouthy with me, man, and you won't get nothing."

Raider sneered at him. "But when I get loose, *man*, you'll get plenty."

"I kinda hope you do at that. 'Cause I want you all for myself."

"Then let's hope we both get what we want, Willie."

Willie reached into his coat pocket—Raider would have been willing to rob a nun for five minutes' possession of that coat—and pulled out a beer bottle. He uncapped it and put the brown bottle into Raider's other hand.

"I want a blanket," Raider said. Now that he seemed to be on a roll there was no point in being shy.

"No blanket," Willie said. He cocked his head to one side and grimaced. "We got to keep you alive, but it don't matter by how much. Fact is, we'll be doing you a favor, man, if we let you die now. Nicest thing I could do for you'd be to give you your fire by settin' this whole place afire. That'd kill you quick. Time she gets here, you'll sure as hell wish you was dead."

Willie turned and walked out of the shack, pulling his coat collar high against the cut of the wind as he stepped outside.

Only when he was gone did Raider take the first welcome swallow from the bottle of beer and the first luxurious taste from the boiled beef sandwich.

She?

Willie had said when *she* got there.

So who the fuck was this *she* person?

CHAPTER THIRTY-SEVEN

Weatherbee fidgeted. There wasn't as much snow in the air as there had been through much of the day, but the wind was just as bad, perhaps even worse now. The still-falling snow and that that had come down earlier in the day were both being blown along the ground and built into deep drifts wherever the wind chose to drop it.

Doc stood in relative comfort at the mouth of the mine tunnel—the Ute girl's "cave"—and fretted while he watched.

He should have been content enough. Between them he and the girl had brought in wood enough to last them for days. At his back she had a fire blazing comfortably, radiating heat from wall to wall inside the low tunnel. A good meal lay warm in his stomach, and if the storm continued for days to come, he and the girl would be safe here.

But Doc felt uneasy. An irrational sense of urgency kept goading him.

He turned his back on the wind that was sweeping past the mouth of the old shaft and went back to stand beside the girl at the fire. He pulled his coat open to let the heat of it reach him. Jane was kneeling beside the fire, adding wood to it. Idly he put a hand on her shoulder and patted her.

Misunderstanding, the girl bobbed her head in instant agreement, stood, and began to pull her dress off over her head. She was still scrawny. It would take much more than the few meals Doc had given her to round out that slat-thin figure and bring some vitality to her.

She was not quite so discomforting to look at now, though. The mud ball had fallen off her nose during the day. The dark, ugly wounds where her former tribesmen had split her nostrils was scabbed over. The wounds were much less distracting than the lump of mud had been. Besides, Doc was used to it now. He hardly noticed the scabs any longer.

"That . . . isn't what I meant," he said awkwardly.

She stopped, the leather dress dangling from her hand, and stood waiting for instruction. It was obvious that she would do whatever he required.

It was just as obvious to him, though, that she had no desires of her own in the matter. If he took her it would be just that—a usage of her body and not a thing in which two people participated. Only one of them could reach any measure of enjoyment, and to him that meant neither of them really could.

He shook his head and said, "Put your dress back on, Jane."

Without any change in her expression, the girl began to pull her dress back on.

Doc sighed. "Get your coat, too. And the packs. The storm is letting up. I have to go on before it gets too dark to travel and those drifts get so deep that we can't move."

The girl looked frightened. "No. Can't. Very bad to go now."

"I have to," Doc said gently. "Of course you don't have come. You could stay here. I'll leave some food for you and a blanket. If I can I shall come back. But I make no promises about that. I hope you understand.

"No." She threw the dress aside and dropped to her knees, clutching at Doc's hands and kissing his palms frantically. "Stay. You must stay here. Please."

She continued to plead with him. With one hand she fondled and felt his crotch, trying to arouse him so that he would be willing to remain in exchange for the pleasures of her body.

In spite of himself, Doc felt a surge of desire. Not only sexual desire but also a desire to comfort and protect this lost, unhappy girl.

He looked beyond her to the swirling snow outside the tunnel. The wind was still driving loose snow in a ground blizzard out there.

It really would be safer to wait until the wind died and the drifts were fully developed.

Jane fumbled with his fly, trying to pull the unfamiliar buttons free.

Doc reached down and patted the naked girl's shoulder with slow, gentling strokes.

CHAPTER THIRTY-EIGHT

Two of them came in, Willie again and the cowboy, whose name Raider did not know. The cowboy looked nervous. Willie looked matter-of-fact. They were carrying chunks of wood, and Raider's first thought was that they were going to beat him with those.

Neither of them came near him, though. In fact, neither of them hardly looked in his direction. Instead they were concentrating on the floor between the open doorway and the post where Raider was chained.

"Here, I think," Willie said. He pointed to one of the areas where the plank flooring had fallen away to expose the rock and gravel underneath and the also rotting joists.

The cowboy grunted and bent to begin clearing the old planking away, clearing a bare and open area.

Raider couldn't figure that. But then he couldn't figure much of what had been happening ever since these bastards descended on Lucinda's place down in New Mexico.

The snow had stopped now, and the last hint of daylight lay outside the door. There was very little for the two to work by.

The snow had stopped, and the wind was dying, but it didn't feel any warmer to Raider. He wasn't sure but thought he might be about at the end of his rope. He was numb all over, not even shivering very much anymore. Just standing there naked in the cold and not feeling much of anything at all.

"I can't see worth a shit," the cowboy complained.

"I'll fetch a lantern." Willie left, turning right toward

the other buildings in the abandoned camp.

"Whuh..." Raider had to work his jaw a bit and try again before he could get the words to form correctly. "What are you shitfaces up to now?"

The cowboy pretended he hadn't heard and continued to pull up pieces of rotten plank and lay them aside.

Willie was back in a few minutes with a lighted lantern. The thing looked brand-new, so they must have packed it in with them. Willie set the lantern on the floor above the hole, and the cowboy went back to his work while Willie watched.

Raider resumed his efforts to increase his circulation, deliberately pulling at the chain and manacles despite the pain it cost him, flexing his legs, moving back and forth to the extent of the chain. Something was happening. Whatever it was he wanted to be prepared to take advantage of any opportunity he might get.

Because if he did get one, it was looking like there wouldn't be time for a second to come after it. Both men were halfway acting like he was already dead.

The cowboy cleared an area about five feet square, then he and Willie began piling small pieces of wood into a pyramid on the hard ground.

They were building a fire, by damn. For once Raider wished them well at the job. He could stand the thought of having a fire to warm up by.

Outside the shack he could hear someone moving about, feet crunching into the snow and voices too low for him to make out. The sounds came nearer, but the other men were not coming to the cabin. They were meeting someone.

"We didn't think you'd make it through." The voice was that of the big, bearded leader of the group, the man without a name.

"Wasn't easy, but we made 'er." The answering voice was an unfamiliar one.

Raider heard the thin clink of bits and chains and the creak of saddle leather.

"Hurry up an' get it lit," Willie hissed.

The cowboy knelt and struck a match. The kindling he had prepared took hold quickly, a small flame spreading and rising to engulf larger and larger pieces of wood until the whole pile was ablaze.

Within seconds Raider could feel the heat of it. He moved as close to the fire as he could, turning to bask in the warmth, one side and then the other. Logic told him that there could be rather little benefit from a fire built inside such an open, drafty area. But his senses drank in every bit of that faint heat that they could. That small amount of warmth revived him much more than the food and drink had earlier in the day.

"D'you want to eat first, ma'am?" It was the bearded man's voice again.

"Yes, but I want to see them before I eat. Where are they?" It was a woman's voice, cultured and velvety. If he had ever heard that voice before, Raider did not now remember it.

There was a pause, then the big man said, "There's only the one so far, ma'am. Raider. We'll get Weatherbee for you, though. Quick as we leave here."

"Your wire said—"

"I know, ma'am, but Weatherbee broke off somewhere around Texas Creek. It was only this'un that stayed behind us. Don't you worry, though. We'll get him for you too."

"You don't get your pay until I have both," the woman said. "Remember that."

A man coughed.

"We wouldn't forget that, ma'am."

"See that you don't."

The woman sounded snooty as hell, Raider thought.

It was dark enough now that all he could see outside were faint impressions of movement. Then the woman reached the doorway and the glow of the lantern and of the fire.

She was dressed like one of the fancy, high-society females that Weatherbee liked. Long gown. Fur trim on her cape. Dressed like she was going to a grand ball and had just stepped out of her carriage, though Raider knew for certain sure that no carriage would ever get within fifty miles of this godforsaken hole in the ground.

She was even wearing a ducky little fur cap and had her

hands stuck into a matching fur muff. The bitch must have ridden the whole way in by sidesaddle, because no woman dressed like that could ever fork a horse.

She was in her thirties, likely, or a damn well-preserved fortyish. Blond hair. Dark eyes. A blush to her cheeks that could have been either the weather or a discreet touch of artificial color.

Raider had never seen her before. He was almost sure of that.

The woman stepped inside, looked down her nose at Willie and the cowboy, and with a flick of her finger motioned them out of the shack. They left in a hurry.

She held her muff in one hand and gathered the skirts of her gown in the other as she stepped carefully around the fire to stand in front of Raider—but carefully outside the reach of a kick—and stared him up and down.

She looked... smug. It took him a while to identify it, but that was what it was. Smug.

She looked first into his eyes, then slowly down toward his bare feet and back up again, settling finally on his crotch.

Raider had been cold-shriveled to begin with. He damn sure hadn't been horny in quite a while. But there was something in this woman's face, something in the depths of her eyes and the cold set of her jaw, that made him draw up even smaller.

Apparently she noticed the reaction because she looked into his eyes again and laughed. He didn't like the sound of that laugh. It scared him the way nothing the gang had done ever might have accomplished.

"The great man's most prized possession," the woman said.

"What?"

"You can't hide anything from me, Raider. I know all about you, everything there is to know. I know what your most valued pleasures are." There was that laugh again as she pointed. Raider's pecker and balls contracted so far they almost pulled inside his body.

"You love to defame innocent girls," the woman accused.

"Are you out of your fucking mind?" Raider was not really cursing her. He was genuinely interested.

"I know all about it, Raider. You have nothing to hide from me." She laughed again. This time he thought the sound was evil and quite possibly deranged as well.

"Before you die, Raider, I intend to take away from you that which you value most. Just as you took from me that which I most loved and valued in this world." Slowly she began to remove one glove, tugging prissily at the tips of each finger in turn. She stepped to the side, still out of reach of a kick, and moved closer.

"I am going to take this away from you, Raider." She reached out to lightly touch his cock, then fingered his scrotum. "I think I shall put this in a jar of pickling salts and set it on my mantel. And these will make a lovely pouch for me to carry my diamonds in." She laughed. "Do you see the humor in that, Raider? I shall carry my stones where you used to carry yours."

"You *are* mad," he said. "Stark, fuckin' raving."

"William assures me he can tan the pouch for me, you see. And of course I shall have the pleasure of collecting the, um, specimens myself." She smiled at him, a cold and awful expression. "Think about that while I go have my dinner, Raider." She pulled her glove back on and pushed her hands into the muff. "I shan't be long, Raider. Wait for me."

Without another word she turned and swept out of the shack, leaving a nearly paralyzed Raider behind her.

Whoever this woman was, and whatever he might have done to piss her off, the bitch was a damned lunatic.

That knowledge did not bring him any comfort at all.

CHAPTER THIRTY-NINE

Blood ran down his arms, dripping off his elbows and making the floor slippery underfoot. The blood came from his wrists, where the steel cuffs bit into them as he tried to wrench the post free of its spikes at the top. If he could do that, he could possibly snatch it up out of the hole into which the lower end was placed. He would still be chained to the damned thing, the chain running through the hole that had been bored through the body of the post, but if he could get it free, maybe...

He did not really know what he might be able to do. He had not looked that far ahead. One thing at a time.

One thing he had *not* done. He had not quit. He had not given up hope. And as long as he breathed he *would* not.

If he could get the post free of the shack he could... hell, he could use it as a battering ram maybe. Club that crazy female to death if he had to. And then worry about the men who were with her.

They were all only paid hands anyway. That was pretty plain from what he'd overheard when she arrived. So if he he could take the source of their pay away from them...

No, that was not very realistic. They might not be bright, some of them anyway, but they wouldn't be idiot enough to think they could do this to him and walk away from it.

There wouldn't be any bullshit about shaking hands and letting bygones be bygones. Not after this. Raider wanted those bastards just as much now as he ever had.

But first he wanted *loose*.

He threw his whole weight backward, flinging himself out to the full length of the short chain, trying desperately to wrest the heavy spikes free of their confinement at the upper end of the stout post.

The pain of the steel cutting into his wrists brought a groan to his lips, and he staggered. He would have fallen to his knees if the chain had not held him upright.

Grimly, determined, Raider regained his balance and poised for another assault on the spikes.

He heard a low chuckle from the direction of the doorway and turned to see the woman standing there.

She looked amused. There was a thin smile on her rouged lips.

She was not carrying the muff now. Instead she had a small, velvet handbag that perfectly matched the collar of her dress that he could see beneath her cape.

Behind her were Bray and Willie.

"I shall enjoy this, Raider. You can't know how very much I shall enjoy this." She entered the decaying shack like a queen entering her throne room and motioned imperiously toward the fire. The big man known as Bray hurried to replenish the fuel so that the flames licked higher.

Raider began to sweat. But that had nothing to do with the scant warmth from the fire.

The woman surveyed the room, seemed satisfied, and unbuttoned her cape. She shrugged out of it and handed the garment to Willie.

Willie, not being trained in the niceties of servitude, did not know what to do with the thing. He looked perplexed for a moment, then dropped the handsome cape—which probably was worth a year's pay for a workingman—into a dusty corner of the shack.

"I shall want him properly trussed," the woman commanded. "Hands behind and around the post. Feet the same, if you please." There was no "if you please" to it. That would only be habit.

"Yes'm," big Bray said. He tossed a last chunk of wood onto the fire and shuffled toward Raider, motioning for Willie to join him.

"You jus—"

Raider interrupted whatever Bray might have said with a swift, slashing kick toward the big man's groin. Bray twisted aside in time to avoid having his cods turned to mush, but Raider's foot landed hard on his thigh and the big man cried out in pain. "Damn you!"

Willie grabbed up a length of hard pine and leaped forward to help subdue the chained but not immobile Raider.

The chain was far too short to allow Raider to dodge out of the way, but he was able to turn and duck his head. The chunk of wood smashed down on the pad of thick muscle across his shoulders. That was preferable to the original target, which had been his head. The blow would have brained him if it had gone where Willie intended.

Bray, cursing viciously, pummeled Raider's side and kidneys as Raider continued to twist and writhe and at the same time tried to land a disabling kick or two on his tormentors.

Past Willie's shoulder he could see the woman, still smiling thinly, as she opened her handbag and reached inside.

She brought out a straight razor and flicked the blade open.

Firelight reflected on the polished steel. Raider stopped his struggles for a moment, fascinated by the sight of the razor in much the same way a viper's weaving head will fascinate and immobilize the bird that will become it's next prey.

Bray's foot lashed out, chopping Raider behind the knee and bringing him down to arm's length, suspended from the chain and handcuffs.

And helpless.

The woman smiled.

CHAPTER FORTY

Doc was beginning to think Jane had been right. They should have stayed back at her "cave." The drifts were worse than he ever would have guessed, and the horse would have been completely played out before now if they hadn't come across the fresh-broken trail they were now following.

Those tracks, barely drifted and therefore quite fresh, led either to shelter or to the gang Raider was chasing, Doc reasoned. He had no idea which it would turn out to be, but he was willing to accept either.

If it was the gang, Raider was probably somewhere behind.

Weatherbee thought about stopping here to wait for Raider to catch up. The two of them would have a much better chance against four armed men than one.

A look back toward the girl, struggling along through the deep snow with her tired horse dragging behind, convinced him otherwise.

If there was shelter of any kind up ahead she needed to reach it.

Not nearly as strong or well fed as he—and he was having some degree of difficulty himself in these unpleasant conditions—the girl's health would be seriously endangered if he did not soon find her warmth and shelter.

So he would press on and just hope that Raider could catch up to them.

The trail of hoof-churned snow led through the narrow valley and up, into a low pass between two of the sharper, higher mountains Doc had seen in this part of the country. It was impossible for him to be sure with the blanket of snow over everything, but he thought they were changing vegetation zones again, leaving the greener but no less rugged country to the north and returning to the arid mountains such as were down along the Arkansas.

Doc climbed into the pass on foot, allowing his horse the rest it badly needed after breaking miles of deep snow and bucking drift after ever deeper drift to reach this point. If the girl only knew of another cave or shaft...

He stopped to rest for a moment and to let the girl catch up to him. "Do you know what's ahead?"

She nodded eagerly, animation lighting her features for practically the first time since they had left the safety of the old tunnel. "White man caves. Houses. People all gone but caves there. And wood. We can stop there?"

"I think so."

White man caves, houses, people all gone. That would be one of the many ghost camps that dotted this country, abandoned when the gold or silver ores played out and there was no more reason for men to endure the crude existence of these mountains.

Abandoned, though. People all gone. So the tracks they were following would not have been left by someone on his way home after a trip to the railroad for supplies.

That almost certainly meant that he was closing in on the gang.

And still no sign of Raider.

Doc thought once again about waiting here for Raider to catch up and join them.

But he had to get the girl to shelter. There was nothing here that he could see.

He certainly could not wait until morning if he was going to have to take them on by himself. In daylight they might have sentries posted. If anyone looked, they and their horses would be all too plainly visible.

No, he decided, better to try and take them now, before they could have any warning that they were not alone here.

Besides, with luck he might be able to catch them unawares and take them peacefully.

"Let's go," Doc told the girl. "But you stay back. There could be trouble up ahead, and I wouldn't want you to get hurt." He gave her the reins of his horse, pulled his rifle from the scabbard slung on his saddle, and went ahead on foot while the Ute girl followed with both animals and all their gear.

CHAPTER FORTY-ONE

"Shit, he's out, lady. Scairt so bad he's passed out cold."

"Then prepare him the way I wish while you can. You can bring him around when we are ready."

"You're really gonna do this, lady?"

"I do not pay so much for nothing, little man."

"Yes, ma'am."

Raider heard them moving about close in front of him. He could not see. Perhaps that was just as well. He put all of his concentration into keeping his face slack and expressionless and into keeping his breathing slow and steady. They would be more cautious if they realized that he was not unconscious. And he wanted to allow them all the lack of caution they wanted.

Strong hands grabbed his wrists and pulled him up, taking his dead weight off the chain to create some slack. The man who was holding him up had to be Bray. He could feel the man's breath in his face and could smell liquor on it.

The other man, Willie, grunted and grumbled behind him. "Gotta undo every-damn-thing...here...an'...start all over." There was a pause and a very faint metallic sound. "There. Hold him now, Bray. Don't let him down quite yet. I gotta get this thing loose. Just a minute now. I almost got it."

There was the soft, dull sound of metal chain links rubbing across wood, gathering speed quickly, and the free end of the chain fell down to give Raider a nasty crack on the back of his head.

178

The chain was free of the post. It was more than Raider had dared hope for.

Raider let out an earsplitting roar, directly into Bray's startled face.

The big man's grip loosened, and Raider yanked his wrists away from the man.

The chain, open padlock dangling from it, swooshed wickedly through the air.

Raider's hands were still cuffed together, but he was no longer chained to the post. And the chain itself was all the weapon he asked for.

Hands clamped together, Raider whirled the chain over his head once to give it momentum and then slashed the links across Bray's eyes before the big man could react.

He didn't wait to see what damage he had done but continued the quick, catlike motion into a spin, twisting, bringing the flying chain back under control even before he spotted Willie.

The little gunman was fast. Raider had to give him that. Even as Raider turned to meet him, Willie's hand was flashing toward his holster.

But the butt of the revolver was encumbered by the tail of Willie's coat and he had to fumble for it, losing precious half seconds as he did so.

By the time Willie could get a grip on the gun, Raider was already swinging the chain.

He drove the steel links hard across Willie's knuckles, sending the blued steel Colt flying.

Willie's eyes got wide, and he stood rooted in sudden fear as Raider whipped the chain back again, smashing it across the smaller man's throat and driving him to his knees. Willie's larynx was crushed, and he went down gagging for breath that he would not in this life be able to achieve.

Bray was back on his feet, blood streaming down his face from a gash along his cheek and temple wide enough to show the pink-tinged white of bone.

Raider swung the chain again, driving Bray back against the wall with his arms upraised in a futile effort for protection.

The chain bit into Bray's flesh again and again, over and over, cutting, slicing, until both men were covered with blood.

Raider continued to beat the whimpering man, his own senses overcome with his rage, until the sounds of gunshots outside the shack stopped him and brought him back to an awareness of his continued danger.

He was naked and blood-spattered and manacled. And somewhere out there were a number of men who were rapists and killers and worse. And somewhere along with them a woman whose complete viciousness frightened him.

He left Bray alone and found Willie's Colt where it had fallen on the floor.

There was no sign of the woman in the shack now. Raider had never known when she fled, but she was gone now. He had neither seen nor heard her go.

The feel of the Colt was good in his hand. He held on to it and pulled Bray's rust-specked Smith and Wesson from the big man's holster too, giving him a dozen shots if he needed them.

The Smith did not feel nearly as good to him. The grip shape and the set of the hammer were awkward for fast use. But the revolvers were accurate even if awkward. Probably Bray, big as he was, had never had to rely on speed when he fought. Muscle would have been his style.

Wouldn't be anymore, Raider realized as he bent over the still form of the man they had called Bray. The chain had ripped the side of Bray's neck open, and now the body lay in a still spreading pool of bright, copper-smelling blood. If Bray was not dead yet he would be within minutes. Raider didn't even try to feel sorry for the death or for the way it had come about. Bray was one of the men who had forced himself on Lucinda.

"All right," Raider hissed.

He blew out the lantern—there was nothing he could do about the fire at the moment, and anyway he still needed the little heat it could give—and went to the door of the shack.

The clouds must have blown off, because there was moonlight bringing a pale glow to the white spread of snow on the ground. It wasn't much light, but it was enough to let him distinguish dark forms here and there.

There was what looked like a body lying off to his right, face down in the snow. Judging from the hat it might have been the cowboy.

Who or what had killed him Raider did not yet know.

He saw a figure break from the cover of a building forty or so yards to his left. The figure scuttled toward him, pausing once to fire a pistol shot into the darkness on the far side of the creek that had created this gulch.

There was an answering spit of flame from behind a boulder over there.

Both shots missed their targets, and the man on this side of the creek lumbered to the shack where Raider waited.

Still looking out into the darkness, the man backed inside the shack and leveled his revolver across the creek. He plainly was aware of Raider immediately behind him. Just as plainly he was assuming that the man who stood near him was Willie or Bray.

"It's that sonuvabitch Weatherbee," the bearded, no-name man said. "I got a clear look at him. Sonuvabitch. Don't know how he found us. But it'll save us the work o' looking for him, eh?" He chuckled and cocked his revolver.

"Yeah," Raider said. "Sure will save us some trouble."

The bearded man's head jerked around and his eyes got wide with recognition. "You! But—"

"It's a pisser, ain't it?" Raider fired the .44-caliber Smith and Wesson point-blank into the bearded man's right ear. The shape of the man's head changed, and Raider was aware of the strong stench as the dead man's bowels voided. The bearded man was dead long before he hit the ground.

Down to Raider's right there were two guns firing now. And Doc shooting back from across the creek.

Weatherbee got one of them. Raider could hear the shriek of pain and the fall of the body onto a wooden floor.

And then there was only one gun firing.

Raider leaned out of his doorway and shouted, "Here. Rally here, boys." He hoped to hell that damned Weatherbee recognized his voice. Or at least was shooting poorly tonight.

Alonzo answered Raider's summons. The man obligingly dashed out of the building where he had holed up and headed in the direction he had seen his boss go a few moments earlier. "Cover me, boys, cover me," he yelled as he ran. Weatherbee took a shot at him but missed.

"You're covered," Raider said dryly as Alonzo skidded inside the shack into the light of the fire.

"Oh, shit."

"Yeah," Raider agreed. He shot Alonzo twice, once with each revolver, and watched the man crumple to the floor.

Raider went back to the doorway and leaned out. He was shivering again from the cold, although damned if he hadn't completely forgotten about it for a while there.

"Hey, Weatherbee."

"Is that you, Rade?"

"Hell yes it's me."

"I thought you were behind me."

"That'll be the day." Raider's teeth were chattering, and he was feeling weak-kneed from the cold and lack of food. "Careful, Doc. There's some crazy-assed woman around here looking to kill people. You and me in particular."

"No," a voice said practically in his ear. Raider almost jumped out of his skin at the sound. This weird-looking Indian girl was standing there. She had a bum nose and was wearing a mighty familiar-looking cape with fur trim on it. And there seemed to be quite a bit of blood on her and the cape both. She was cleaning the blade of a knife on the fine woolen fabric of the cape. "Woman, she have a razor?"

"Yeah, that's the one."

"Not very good fighter, that one." The girl smiled at him.

"Weatherbee?" His voice did not come out nearly as

loud as he wanted it to. He staggered and tried to make it to the fire so he could get warm for the first time in he didn't know how long.

The girl had to help him the last few steps of the way. Outside he could hear Doc running across the snow to join them.

CHAPTER FORTY-TWO

"I've no idea who she is. Was," Weatherbee corrected himself. He knelt and took another look at the pale, bloodless face of the woman who had caused all this.

In death she looked fifteen years older than she had before, Raider thought. Hard now and not at all attractive. Not that he had exactly been attracted to her to begin with. But he at least had been able to see in her a certain quality of style. And of evil. That was gone too now. Now she seemed shrunken and forlorn in the ungainly sprawl of the violently dead.

Weatherbee examined the dead woman. Raider looked her over closely again. The Ute girl whom they called Jane ignored the body after a brief experiment proved the live girl could not make use of the dead woman's fashionable boots.

Doc shook his head. "I'm sure I've never seen her before," he said.

"Me neither, but she damn sure had something against us. Had to be something pretty potent to call for all this."

"Hatred and a great deal of money, too," Doc said.

"You'd sure as hell think we'd remember if we'd done anything that awful to her," Raider said.

Doc looked down at the woman sadly, then turned and picked up the handbag that had fallen nearby during the woman's final struggle with Jane.

The girl pressed close against his side, partially for the reassurance of his presence but also looking quite frankly into the open top of the purse. She obviously was curious about the things that a white lady might carry with her in such an odd contraption as a velvet purse.

Weatherbee pulled out a clean lace handkerchief and a soiled one. A small, flat jar that the girl immediately appropriated from him—it was some sort of cream lotion with a scent of spring flowers, soon liberally slathered over the Ute girl's cheeks and neck—and a largish purse that held currency in one pocket and coins in the other. Jane seemed interested in the coins but not the currency.

"Wait just a minute here," Doc said. He dipped once again into the handbag and came up with a small leather case.

"Calling cards?"

"Yes."

Weatherbee pulled one out. He made a face as he read it, then handed the card to Raider.

"So?" Raider asked. "Marguerite Bellon-Smythe. Big deal. Or is that s'posed to mean something?"

"Quite a lot, actually." Weatherbee pulled an Old Virginia from his pocket, bit off the tip, and lighted the cheroot. The girl reached inside his coat and helped herself to one also, which he lighted for her.

"I don't know what in hell you're talking about, Doc. The name don't mean anything to me."

"It should." Weatherbee drew on his cheroot for a moment, then with a sigh reminded Raider of the connection.

"Last year," Doc said, "there was this case with Jonas Bellon. You remember him, don't you?"

"Hell yes. Fat-cat industrialist with big ideas. Except that he was stealing from his stockholders and putting the cash in his own pockets. The way I remember it, we never actually pulled him in, though."

"That's right. The man committed suicide before we could get to him. We had no more than gotten warrants issued for his arrest than he took the easy way out."

"Right. So what's that got to do with this?" Raider asked.

"Bellon was a married man. But we knew he had a mistress on the side. Someone he was awfully fond of."

Raider looked down toward the dead woman. "Her?"

"I suspect so," Doc said. "You told me she made a claim about us taking everything away from her. Everything of value."

Raider made a face. "Not that ugly SOB. Couldn't no woman get excited over him."

"No, but a woman certainly could be that excited about his money. Or even more important, about the social position a marriage to Jonas Bellon would have brought her. If, that is, he had not been exposed and ruined. Think about that, Rade."

"I don't know, Doc."

"Look at her clothes, the fact that she was carrying engraved calling cards, the way she carried herself, if you were telling me things accurately. A very haughty woman, I should say. And there is the fact that she changed her name to Bellon-Smythe. The rumor then was that Bellon was keeping some woman named Smith, but we always assumed it was an obvious alias to keep her identity hidden. Not that we cared to look for her anyway. She was guilty of no crimes that I knew of except in her judgment."

Raider looked down toward the dead woman again. "I'm still almighty suspicious of her judgment, Doc." He felt a small indrawing of protest deep in his groin at the thought of what nearly happened to him at this woman's hand.

"Um," Weatherbee muttered around the end of his cigar. "Difficult not to, eh?"

"You said it."

Doc sighed. "We have some work to do to get this mess cleaned up. Will you be going down to New Mexico when we get done?"

Raider stared off toward the starlit sky. "I don't know, Doc." His voice was close to a whisper. A whisper of concern and perhaps a tinge of wistfulness, too. "It could've been good down there, Doc. But..." He didn't finish. Whatever he might have said, he did not.

"I know, Rade," Doc said gently. But he did not.

The two men walked back to the warmth of the fire, the slender Ute girl close at Weatherbee's side. And no one at all close to Raider. It was a loss Raider recognized and all too keenly felt.

"THE MOST EXCITING WESTERN WRITER SINCE LOUIS L'AMOUR"
—JAKE LOGAN

___	06412-3	BOUNTY HUNTER #31	$2.50
___	07700-4	CARNIVAL OF DEATH #33	$2.50
___	08013-7	THE WYOMING SPECIAL #35	$2.50
___	07257-6	SAN JUAN SHOOTOUT #37	$2.50
___	07259-2	THE PECOS DOLLARS #38	$2.50
___	07114-6	THE VENGEANCE VALLEY #39	$2.75
___	07386-6	COLORADO SILVER QUEEN #44	$2.50
___	07790-X	THE BUFFALO SOLDIER #45	$2.50
___	07785-3	THE GREAT JEWEL ROBBERY #46	$2.50
___	07789-6	THE COCHISE COUNTY WAR #47	$2.50
___	07974-0	THE COLORADO STING #50	$2.50
___	08032-3	HELL'S BELLE #51	$2.50
___	08088-9	THE CATTLETOWN WAR #52	$2.50
___	08669-0	THE TINCUP RAILROAD WAR #55	$2.50
___	07969-4	CARSON CITY COLT #56	$2.50
___	08743-3	THE LONGEST MANHUNT #59	$2.50
___	08774-3	THE NORTHLAND MARAUDERS #60	$2.50
___	08792-1	BLOOD IN THE BIG HATCHETS #61	$2.50
___	09089-2	THE GENTLEMAN BRAWLER #62	$2.50
___	09112-0	MURDER ON THE RAILS #63	$2.50
___	09300-X	IRON TRAIL TO DEATH #64	$2.50
___	09213-5	HELL IN THE PALO DURO #65	$2.50
___	09343-3	THE ALAMO TREASURE #66	$2.50
___	09396-3	BREWER'S WAR #67	$2.50
___	09480-4	THE SWINDLER'S TRAIL #68	$2.50
___	09568-1	THE BLACK HILLS SHOWDOWN #69	$2.50
___	09648-3	SAVAGE REVENGE #70	$2.50
___	09714-5	TRAIN RIDE TO HELL #71	$2.50

Available at your local bookstore or return this form to:

THE BERKLEY PUBLISHING GROUP
Berkley • Jove • Charter • Ace
THE BERKLEY PUBLISHING GROUP, Dept. B
390 Murray Hill Parkway, East Rutherford, NJ 07073

Please send me the titles checked above. I enclose _____. Include $1.00 for postage and handling if one book is ordered; add 25¢ per book for two or more not to exceed $1.75. CA, IL, NJ, NY, PA, and TN residents please add sales tax. Prices subject to change without notice and may be higher in Canada. Do not send cash.

NAME_____
ADDRESS_____
CITY_____ STATE/ZIP_____
(Allow six weeks for delivery.)

Explore the exciting Old West with one of the men who made it wild!

__08965-6	LONGARM #1	$2.75
__08063-2	LONGARM ON THE SANTE FE #36	$2.50
__08069-0	LONGARM AND THE COMANCHEROS #38	$2.50
__07414-4	LONGARM IN THE BIG THICKET #48	$2.50
__07854-9	LONGARM IN THE BIG BEND #50	$2.50
__08099-3	LONGARM AND THE OUTLAW LAWMAN #56	$2.50
__07858-1	LONGARM IN NO MAN'S LAND #58	$2.50
__07886-7	LONGARM AND THE BIG OUTFIT #59	$2.50
__08259-7	LONGARM AND SANTA ANNA'S GOLD #60	$2.50
__08388-7	LONGARM AND THE CUSTER COUNTY WAR #61	$2.50
__06267-7	LONGARM AND THE HANGMAN'S NOOSE #66	$2.50
__08331-3	LONGARM ON THE GOODNIGHT TRAIL #80	$2.50
__08343-7	LONGARM AND THE FRONTIER DUCHESS #81	$2.50
__08367-4	LONGARM IN THE BITTERROOTS #82	$2.50
__08445-X	LONGARM AND THE BIG SHOOT-OUT #85	$2.50
__08495-6	LONGARM AND THE TEXAS PANHANDLE #87	$2.50
__08569-3	LONGARM AND THE ISLAND PASSAGE #89	$2.50

Available at your local bookstore or return this form to:

 JOVE
THE BERKLEY PUBLISHING GROUP, Dept. B
390 Murray Hill Parkway, East Rutherford, NJ 07073

Please send me the titles checked above. I enclose _____ Include $1.00 for postage and handling if one book is ordered; add 25¢ per book for two or more not to exceed $1.75. CA, IL, NJ, NY, PA, and TN residents please add sales tax. Prices subject to change without notice and may be higher in Canada. Do not send cash.

NAME_____

ADDRESS_____

CITY_____ STATE/ZIP_____

(Allow six weeks for delivery.)

Alfonso Vasseur Walls
José Ramos Cervantes

Diccionario
ESPAÑOL
INGLÉS

INGLÉS
ESPAÑOL

Nueva edición actualizada que incluye:
- una lista completa de verbos irregulares ingleses.
- un moderno vocabulario inglés-español de términos comerciales y financieros.

EDITORIAL DIANA
MEXICO

1a. Edición, Agosto de 1957
53a. Impresión, Junio de 2005

DERECHOS RESERVADOS
©

ISBN 968-13-0910-3

Copyright © 1957 por Editorial Diana, S.A. de C.V.
Arenal No. 24, Edif. Norte,
Ex Hacienda Guadalupe Chimalistac,
01050, México, D.F.
www.diana.com.mx

IMPRESO EN MÉXICO – PRINTED IN MEXICO

Prohibida la reproducción total o parcial
sin autorización por escrito de la casa editora.